MW01119652

LIBERTY

A Play

Dyanna Morrison

With Gratitude

It's been a little over a year since I started on my journey to transition my stage play Justice, and now, Liberty, into books. I've learned a lot over the last year and I am grateful for the professional relationships that I have forged along the way that have resulted in my ability to bring these stories to life in the written format. I remain hopeful that as we emerge from the coronavirus pandemic that my works will once again have the opportunity to be performed on stage!

The mechanics of self-publishing a book was not second nature to me. As with everything, it takes teamwork and I have had the good fortune to be able to collaborate on Liberty with the same team that I worked with on Justice.

I continue to get a lot of compliments on the great cover/artwork for Justice and that same team has continued to be great to work with in preparing the covers/artwork for Liberty. My continued thanks to: Cover Design:SelfPubBookCovers.com/RLSather.

I also need to give a huge round of thanks and appreciation to Brenda VanNiekerk of http://triomarketers.com. Brenda has proven to be a professional book formatting aficionado and a wealth of knowledge regarding all facets of self-publishing in general. She has gone above and beyond to provide assistance in many areas where I needed guidance. I wholeheartedly recommend anyone looking to self-publish to reach out to these professional providers for further details.

Lastly, I must again thank my dear Uncle Norm, for putting this story in my head in the late 90's! Those were the best of lunches and the best of conversations in a friendship I coveted! I will miss you always!

Contents

FOREWORD

Is there a more combustible and divisive issue than gun control versus gun rights in our national debate currently? Since I started writing this foreword section in April 2021, mass shooting statistics have changed on a weekly and sometimes daily basis. The message of Liberty has grown even more relevant to our current fight for meaningful gun control reform, then it was when I wrote the first outline back in the early 2000s.

There were just two mass killings in 2020 prior to the lockdown resulting from the coronavirus pandemic. The February 26 event at the Milwaukee Brewery, where the mass shooter killed five co-workers before killing himself and on March 15 when a man killed four people in Springfield, MO, before killing himself. After a year of lock down, large crowds are starting to gather again. Our public gathering places, including schools, churches, workplaces and shopping centers are reopening, reigniting mass shootings and mass killings, which are defined as any event involving four or more people.

2020 was such a tragic year! When the coronavirus pandemic emerged, I'm not sure that anyone could have anticipated that by the spring of 2021, the U.S. would have suffered the passing of 600,000 of our people. Thankfully, the death rate has started to decrease significantly. There could be no silver linings to the haunting year of 2020. As a result of the mandated nationwide lockdown, mass killings decreased significantly, while mass shootings increased by almost 600%, as a result of gang violence, drive by shootings, suicide, and random firearm deaths.

During this year of lock downs, social distancing and remote working arrangements, our environment had a brief respite as a result of this decrease in human activity, public gatherings, and decreases in vehicular and structural carbon emissions. 2020 was a year of civil unrest and economic and political turmoil all wrapped up in a global pandemic.

When you go almost an entire year without daily mass public gatherings of the general populace limiting social exposure, there are less opportunities for mass shooters to threaten normal crowds in public spaces. Unfortunately, our country's resurgence from the coronavirus pandemic has resulted in a resurgence of senseless mass killings. As of May 20, 2021, there had already been nearly 200 mass shootings, picking up at an accelerated pace since the beginning of 2021 and increasing on a daily, weekly, and monthly basis since. Through the years, this has become a typical pattern. Once one mass killing occurs, others follow at a pretty rapid rate, known as the "contagion" or "copycat" effect. Over the last decade, it has become clear that one mass shooting leads to another mass shooting.

A March 25, 2021, NY Times article stated that, "gun violence…kills about 40,000 Americans a year. US states with fewer guns like CA, IL, IA, and much of the Northeast have fewer gun deaths… Mass shootings aren't the main problem…In 2019, only about one out of every 400 gun deaths was the result of a mass shooting. More than half of gun deaths are from suicides." I thought this article was particularly interesting because it further elaborated that, "… the main reason members of Congress feel comfortable blocking gun control is that most Americans don't feel strongly enough about the issue to change their votes because of it. If Americans stopped voting for opponents of gun control, gun-control laws would pass very quickly." So here is another example where it seems that the only way to get Congress to pass meaningful gun legislation is by every single one of us making our voices heard. Only through persistent, repeated efforts, both grass roots and by contacting our legislators, can we reinforce the importance of passing meaningful gun control reform.

The U.S. makes up less than 5% of the world's population but Americans own more than 40% of the estimated civilian owned guns worldwide and is home to over 30% of global mass shooters. It is unfortunate that in the aftermath of mass shootings and mass killings we seem to be able to keep gun control conversations front and center, but nothing ever gets done and we find ourselves repeatedly back to square one.

An April 26, 2021 article by NPR.org. stated that, "the week of March 15-21 was the top week for FBI background checks since 1998, completing 1,218,002 total firearm checks. In January, more than 4 million background checks were processed, compared with the previous January's 2.7 million. And in February 2021, 3.4 million checks were reported; in February 2020, 2.8 million were completed. During the entire month of March 2021, the FBI completed nearly 4.7 million background checks compared with the same month the year before when the agency reported 3.7 million checks," following a string of high-profile mass shootings. The article goes on to quote a gun store owner, who states, "These buyers are white, black, Asian and Latino and come from all political beliefs. And they're driven by uncertainty, fear and a need to feel safe."

Both 2020 and 2021 saw a record increase in the number of gun purchases, especially involving first time buyers, for a myriad of reasons, including: civil unrest across the country as a result of the killing of George Floyd and other killings resulting from police brutality, economic uncertainty in light of the coronavirus pandemic and the rise of white supremacy and white nationalist movements and general political upheaval. Some states witnessed an exponential increase in gun sales during the pandemic, including both the District of Columbia and Michigan, where gun sales increased by 449% and 200% respectively in the August 2019 – August 2020 timeframe.

A November 27, 2020 article by Conversation.com explained that, "With demand for firearms increasing, the FBI's National Instant Criminal Background Checks System (NICS) struggled to keep up and provide sellers with definitive background check decisions within the required time. This legal loophole in the system allowed sellers to use their own discretion to sell (or not) when background checks came back as inconclusive." No background check sales account for an estimated 40% of gun sales in the US. The article further details that, "…1.3 million handguns and 700,000 rifles and shotguns [had been] sold by August 2020. This was an increase of 60% over average US sales, with August gun sales being the fifth highest month on record according to FBI data. Schools, federal buildings and places of worship only account for 25%, 10% and 4% of mass shooter incidents respectively – with commercial and retail premises accounting for almost 50% of attacks."

The lack of oversight and regulation of gun dealers, gun shops and pawnbrokers is another contributing factor to the unchecked availability of guns across the U.S. It is a well-known, ongoing problem and one that has been consistently easy for gun sellers to capitalize on and abuse as a result of unenforced regulations. The Bureau of Alcohol, Tobacco, Firearms and Explosives (ATF), is sorely understaffed and has been without a Director for six years. David Chipman, President Biden's current nominee for the position, remains under intense scrutiny as his Senate approval hearings continue.

Gun sellers continue to take advantage of this lack of regulation. Records are falsified, background checks are not run at all or done incorrectly, proper I.D.'s are not presented, and straw purchases are overlooked. This creates the perfect storm for allowing deadly weapons to get into the hands of convicted felons, domestic abusers, gang members, drug cartels and every other walk of life that should not have access to firearms, including applicants that actually failed their background check.

Despite the fact that a single violation is enough to shut down a gun seller, the ATF only revokes licenses in less than 3% of cases. Gun dealers are supposed to be inspected at least once every three years, but the reality is that they are inspected closer to once every seven years. The long-standing debate regarding, "the gun show loophole," is a bit misleading. The name/reference would infer that it applies to where a gun or guns are being sold, but it actually applies to who is selling the gun/firearms. Gun sellers that are federally licensed must run background checks, but not all sellers are required to be licensed, and find venues like gun shows to be a perfect place to unload their goods. Gun dealers feel emboldened to break the laws because there are no consequences for their actions.

Personally, I do believe that the right to bear arms is an individual right, but not at all a right granted by the Second Amendment. I felt it important to highlight this in Attorney Pantovere's dialogue in Act II. Scene 12. He reminds us that, "The purpose of our Bill of Rights, was to incorporate into our Constitution, a set of rights that the federal government cannot infringe upon. Every amendment in the Bill of Rights is either declaratory or restrictive but none of them grant anybody the right to anything. The right to freedom of speech, freedom of the press, freedom of religion and the right to bear arms are God given rights we are born with, but they are not absolutes and are restricted by the powers given to state governments." Historically, our founding documents deferred to state governments to pass meaningful and timely gun control measures. That is until the U.S. Supreme Court passed down the two verdicts in both Heller and McDonald in 2008 and 2010, respectively. In 2008 the U.S. Supreme Court handed down the Heller decision, declaring that the Second Amendment was in fact, an individual right.

Prior to the Heller ruling, The U.S. Supreme Court's last ruling regarding the Second Amendment was back in 1939, in the United States v. Miller, reversing a district court ruling, siding with Miller, who had been indicted for transporting an unregistered sawed-off shotgun across state lines in violation of the National Firearms Act of 1934. Miller argued that violated his Second Amendment rights and The Western District Court of Arkansas agreed with Miller. The U.S. Supreme Court reversed the district court's decision, stating that, "[in] the absence of any evidence tending to show the possession of use of a [sawed off] shotgun…has some reasonable relationship to the preservation or efficiency of a well-regulated militia, we cannot say that the Second Amendment guarantees the right to keep and bear such an instrument." Until the Heller ruling, the U.S. Supreme Court consistently refused to hear cases involving the right to bear arms letting appellate court rulings stand. Forty-four state constitutions contain some kind of right to bear arms clause, with the oldest dating back to 1776 for North Carolina, Pennsylvania, and Virginia. The six states whose state constitutions do not include such provisions are: California, Iowa, Maryland, Minnesota, New Jersey, and New York.

Fast forward to 2008 in the District of Columbia v. Heller, the U.S. Supreme Court ruled that the right to bear arms is an individual right but the court made sure that the Heller decision could not be interpreted too broadly, saying that the Second Amendment rights are not unlimited. It is not a right to keep and carry any weapon whatsoever.

The right to keep and bear arms was not fully incorporated to the states until 2010 in McDonald v. Chicago. Here, the U.S. Supreme Court held that the Second Amendment applies to the states and reaffirmed its ruling under Heller that the right to keep and bear arms is an individual right guaranteed by the due process clause in the Fourteenth Amendment. This decision overturned U.S. v. Cruikshank where the U.S. Supreme Court held that the Second Amendment is an unincorporated right that applies only to the Federal government and not to the states.

Currently, the U.S. Supreme Court has been sending mixed messages regarding its willingness to get involved in Second Amendment cases. In March 2021, the U.S. Supreme Court declined to take up a series of cases seeking to expand gun rights. The Court rejected ten different appeals despite its conservative majority, upholding its right to stay out of the political fray and allow lower court rulings to stand. Conversely, in April 2021, the Court announced that it will preside over a case pertaining to NY state law that restricts an individual from concealed carry of a handgun in public places. The law requires a resident to prove that he has an "actual and articulable" need to do so, which was upheld by a lower court. After a decade of tragic mass shootings and killings, including the series of back to back events in 2021, both gun control and gun rights proponents will be watching with great interest as to how the court will rule in the fall 2021 term.

In November 2019, the U.S. Supreme Court allowed the families of Sandy Hook victims to proceed with a lawsuit against Remington Arms, the manufacturer/marketer of the Bushmaster AR-15 style rifle that was used by shooter, Adam Lanza, in the 2012 killings. The 2005 federal law that shields gun companies from liability has exceptions, including one allowing lawsuits against a gunmaker or seller that knowingly violates state or federal laws governing how a product is sold or marketed. Specifically, one Remington ad for the AR-15 rifle states, "Consider your man card reissued." Remington Arms subsequently filed bankruptcy in an effort to auction itself off, which would result in claimants being denied compensatory damages owed and slowing down the process, resulting in claimants being relegated to a seat on the committee of unsecured creditors.

In January 2021, the National Rifle Association (NRA) filed bankruptcy in the state of NY, despite its contradictory claims of financial stability, as a response to the 2020 lawsuit filed by the NY state Attorney General seeking to put the NRA out of business for misuse of funds and self-dealing. The NRA's claim to dismiss the case or transfer it to another court was denied and, on the surface, could be construed as a bad faith filing in light of their financial solvency. Established in the state of NY in 1871, the NRA itself backed reasonable gun legislation throughout the 1930s - 1960s, until the 1970s when the NRA formed a PAC to focus on gun rights and opposing gun control. The NRA would eventually grow to be one of the top lobbies in Washington, DC. Also in January 2021, the NRA and Sea Girt LLC, a TX company wholly owned by the NRA, which was coincidentally formed two months prior to the bankruptcy filing, sought to restructure as a TX nonprofit, in an effort to flee the state of NY, and the ramifications posed by the ongoing lawsuit threatening the NRA's existence. On May 11, 2021 the Bankruptcy Court for the Northern District of Texas ruled that the NRA's bankruptcy cases were filed in bad faith and dismissed.

One hundred days + into a newly elected administration, there is once again hope that meaningful gun control legislation will be enacted. On April 8, 2021, President Biden signed a series of executive actions in support of gun control. The actions supported ending the creation of ghost guns, which are homemade or makeshift guns without serial numbers, placing regulations on concealed assault style firearms, publishing a model for states on "red flag" laws and establishing reporting on gun trafficking. There are also two laws that have passed in the House of Representatives that are waiting to be brought to the floor of the Senate. H.R.8 which is legislation to enact universal background checks and H.R.1446 which would close the Charleston loophole. On March 11, 2021, Congressman David Cicilline and Senator Diane Feinstein introduced the Assaults Weapon Ban, seventeen years after the original Assault Weapons Ban expired.

The divisive opinions regarding enacting gun control legislation have never been more pronounced across party lines and have widened considerably over the last several years. According to a May 9, 2021 poll by Pew Research Center, the article states that, "Today, just over half of Americans (53%) say gun laws should be stricter than they currently are, a view held by 81% of Democrats but just 20% of Republicans." This represents a double-digit decline in GOP support since 2019. An August 2019 Politico poll showed that most Republicans would support legislation banning assault-style weapons. What a difference a couple of years can make. Despite the mind-boggling, rapid resurgence and acceleration of mass shootings and mass killings witnessed by our country as we continue to reopen from the coronavirus pandemic, Republicans continue to kill all gun control legislation via the filibuster. As Attorney Pantovere vehemently articulates during his dialogue in Act II. Scene 13, "This isn't right versus left, it is right versus wrong."

It is time for us to come together as Americans and take a stand for the long overdue passing of legislation to support and encourage meaningful gun control measures, which in no way would threaten any individuals Second Amendment right to bear arms. In Act I. Scene 7, in his own words, George Washington is quick to point out that, "When the Second Amendment was ratified in 1791, there was certainly a fair measure of gun control. Regulation was certainly intact, stating who could own firearms." We have to demand more from our duly elected members of Congress and of the Senate, then just thoughts and prayers and hearts going out to the families of the victims of senselessly murdered men, women and children, after the fact, whose only mistake was believing that there is a degree of inherent safety in going about their daily affairs in the communities where they live, work, socialize, worship and go to school. We need to somehow restore faith in the fact that the tenet of domestic tranquility, that is as much a part of our Constitution and Bill of Rights as every other article and amendment, can once more be as central to the principles of American democracy as it was at our founding.

As our country reopens, mass shooters open fire in rapid succession, once more bringing to light the inadequacy of outdated gun control laws in most states. In 2017, after the murder of 58 people attending an outdoor music festival in Las Vegas, conservative talk show personality, Bill O'Reilly, shared the sentiment that such mass casualties were, "the price of freedom." I beg to differ. In no way has the Bill of Rights ever conferred to any citizen of the U.S., the right to infringe upon the rights of others.

I listen to the bipartisan exchanges in Congress currently about how individual liberties are being violated as a response to the global pandemic that continues to hit various countries particularly hard with no sign of subsiding anytime soon, and a race to get vaccines to the world's population. Is it really a violation of someone's liberty to try to enforce safety protocols until the pandemic is under control? As Thomas Jefferson aptly states in Act II. Scene 8, "Without safety there can be no liberty." What about the liberty of the 8 people recently shot and killed in Atlanta and the 10 people shot and killed in Denver? Where was their liberty? Where was their domestic tranquility? In Act II. Scene 10, John Adams echoes this sentiment when he states, "There can be no domestic tranquility in a people that live in constant fear." What about the liberty and domestic tranquility of the 26 children, teachers and administrators murdered at Sandy Hook Elementary School on December 14, 2012? Their families continue to fight for their liberty and for some measure of reasonable gun control legislation to no avail. In my mind, one of the most poignant and thought-provoking quotes in Liberty is in Act II. Scene 1, quoting a tweet by British journalist, Dan Hodges, who in referring to the Sandy Hook mass killings stated, "In retrospect Sandy Hook marked the end of the US gun control debate. Once America decided killing children was bearable, it was over." It is a heartbreaking observation that unfortunately was fatally farsighted and remains spot on nine years later.

An August 15, 2019 survey by the American Psychological Association, "found that more than three-quarters of adults (79%) in the U.S. say they experience stress as a result of the possibility of a mass shooting. Nearly one in three adults (32%) feel they cannot go anywhere without worrying about being a victim of a mass shooting, while just about the same number (33%) say fear prevents them from going to certain places or events. Mass shootings are a public health issue, and we need to take a comprehensive public health approach to understand and devise lasting policy solutions."

Though they are my thoughts and words being spoken by George Washington in Act II. Scene 10, if you take nothing away from reading this play, it is my hope that this thought will resonate with you, "Man, how could we have ever anticipated advances in weaponry that would provide for a single weapon or two to be the equivalent to the attack of a full on infantry assault?" As James Madison further states in his own words in Act I. Scene 7, "I strongly stated that the "character" of the Constitution must be tested by the experience of the future. Laws and institutions must go hand in hand with the progress of the human mind." Common sense should prevail in realizing that their intentions for the safeguards included in the Second Amendment were not absolutes and that they would require redress for the passage and advancements of time. In my mind, it seemed reasonable to further have James Madison reiterate in Act II. Scene 2, that words two and three of the Second Amendment are "well" and "regulated." It doesn't seem so far-fetched, that our framers were mindful of exceptions in penning our founding documents.

It is safe to say that our framers, while clearly recognizing the boundless potential of the America of their creation, could never have been able to foresee just how boundless and sophisticated the advancements in technology and weaponry would be in the 20th century and beyond. However, one thing they fully recognized as far back in time as 1791, during the ratification of the Constitution and Bill of Rights, was their prediction for the potential destructive nature of emerging political parties in conducting the business of our federal government on behalf of its constituents. As echoed in his own words in Act II. Scene 12, Alexander Hamilton professes, "Political factions can be one of the most fatal diseases of popular government." Our founders recognized the inherent dangers of these emerging political parties during the nascent years of our country. The sentiments spoken by our founders regarding the likelihood of factious gridlock in several Acts/Scenes throughout Liberty are largely their own words, serving as a reminder to us in the 21st century, that these prescient concerns during the infancy of our founding are even more prevalent and relevant in today's current political fray.

Our country is more divided now than ever, but I am going to remain optimistic that our democracy is stronger than all of the forces that could threaten its perpetuity. As Benjamin Franklin summarized upon exiting the Constitutional Convention, when being questioned as to the form of government that had been created, he responded, "A republic, if you can keep it." This sentiment is further echoed by John Adams in Act III. Scene 4, when he states, "Remember democracy never lasts long. It soon wastes, exhausts, and murders itself. There never was a democracy yet that did not commit suicide." The sentiments of our founders in that entire scene should be reminders to all of us that our "experiment with democracy" is dynamic and ongoing and is by no means a given. We will have to fight for its existence every day, with the support of our legislators, who need to hear our voices and read our letters in support of putting partisan issues aside to enact sensible gun control legislation. George Washington ends Act II. Scene 12, in his own words, emphatically stating, "The Constitution is the guide which I will never abandon." May his sentiments be a reminder to all of us, that this definitive document of our founding, is the document that our elected politicians swear an oath to uphold and defend.

Characters

Bailiff

Foreperson/Jurors

Television Newscaster

Judge Grace Porter Haverhill

Mitchell Haverhill

Michael Pantovere

Leonard Snayder

Dwayne LaFollett

Jackson Owens

Jason/Waitstaff

Timothy Miller

Sean Hastings

Sarah Pinckney

Robert Ring

George Washington

John Adams

Alexander Hamilton

Thomas Jefferson

James Madison

Aaron Burr

ACT I

DEVASTATION

I.1 INT. JACKSON OWENS LIVING ROOM - NIGHT

> *Jackson Owens, a tall, husky white male is sitting in a dining room chair, hunched over the table. The room is dimly lit. In one hand he holds a pistol, in the other he clutches a framed picture of his now murdered family, his wife and three children. There is a half empty bottle of whiskey on the table. In his desperation, he is playing Russian Roulette.*

JACKIE OWENS

Oh baby, my sweet baby, Sally, oh baby, how can you ever forgive me?

>   (sobbing violently and waving the
>   gun around)

At least you're with them now, our beautiful angels. Oh my Tommy boy, my sweet angel, Alissa and my little doll face, Hailey.

>   (taking a swig of whiskey)

I might as well be dead baby,

(holding the gun to his head)

Cause living without you, without my family is just like being dead. It was all my fault. I had to be such a big man, shooting off my mouth, screaming about my Second Amendment rights. A proud pistol packing member of the "N" fuckin "R' fuckin "A." Please God, take me now.

(he holds the gun to his head and pulls the trigger, resulting in an empty chamber being fired)

I'm begging you to take me now, God! I want to go just the way they went, by the force of a bullet, but in my dumb ass brain. Take me now, so that I can be with them in heaven!

(he points the gun to his head again and pulls the trigger, resulting in an empty chamber being fired, he continues wallowing in his lamentations and takes another swig as he prepares for one more try)

Shit! Even God doesn't want me! Arrogant, ignorant, gun packin, white trash rednecks don't get the chance to walk through those pearly gates!

(he points the gun to his head in misery as he prepares for one more try)

CUT TO:

I.2 EXT. - FLASHBACK TO AN OUTDOOR NRA/PROGUN
RALLY FAIRFAX, VA - DAY

> *The President of the NRA is
> giving a fiery presentation to
> the crowd of a thousand about
> their sacred Second Amendment
> right to bear arms. The crowd
> is divided unequally between
> NRA supporters and gun control
> activists. There are more
> cheers than jeers as he
> continues with his speech.*

DWAYNE LAFOLLETT

My fellow Americans and proud supporters of our
most sacred Second Amendment, thank you for
joining us here today as we make a stand and
united we stand...

(cheers and jeers from the crowd)

To keep and bear arms! I am here to tell our
Congress and all of the gun control special
interest groups to call it a day! Yes, that's
right just turn around and go home with your
tail between your legs and prattle on about your
Utopian society. Yeah, right, it's all peace and
love and everyone gets along.

(raising his voice for emphasis)

What world do you live in? Because it is not the
real world!

(cheers and jeers from the crowd)

We don't all get along and frequently there is
no reason for it. People shoot each other up in

the name of love, in the name of God, in the name of jealousy and infidelity, in the name of road rage, in the name of mental illness and in the name of hunger and oppression. That is the reality we live in! And a well-armed society can defend themselves against those who kill and maim, because they have the constitutional right to do so! There are over 2.5 Million defensive gun usages each year and that number is on the rise. The solution to the crime-infested nation that we live in is not less guns, it is MORE guns! Why gun ownership and our membership has continued to soar over the past 20 years. Isn't that fantastic! Every time there is a mass shooting, gun ownership and our membership sores! Guns are not at the root of our problems; they are the answer to our problems! Thank God for our constitutionally protected guns!

(pauses for effect)

You and all of your families can rest tonight, knowing that you are all safe and secure as your Second Amendment rights are protected. The Trump administration has vowed to make sure those safe-guards continue! GUNS! GUNS! GUNS! We need our GUNS!

> LaFollett is fired up and con-
> tinues to whip up the crowd in a
> frenzy that has both supporters
> and detractors expressing their
> support or lack thereof and the
> security and police are becoming
> more engaged to try to minimize
> the conflict and stop the con-
> frontations that are continuing
> to happen.

                    DWAYNE LAFOLLETT (CONT'D)
That's right, be ever reverent to the power and
peace our GUNS bring us as citizens of these
United States and the laws guaranteed by our
Constitution and the Bill of Rights.

                (pauses for effect)

The Second Amendment says, "A well-regulated
militia, being necessary to the security of a
free state...

                        LaFollett is interrupted by a
                        rapid series of gun shots, as
                        shots are fired into the crowd,
                        indiscriminately and appear to
                        be coming from a window in one
                        of the top floors of a build-
                        ing across the street. There is
                        pandemonium, as the crowd runs
                        for safety and hundreds of people
                        are wounded, with many killed.

                            CUT TO: SIDE WINDOW IN
                                 THE COURTROOM.
                              DISSOLVE THROUGH
                              THE WINDOW TO THE
                               OTHER SIDE TO
                               INTRODUCE THE
                             INITIAL FLASHBACK
                               SCENE, 1790'S:

I.3 INT. - "THE RED ROOM" WHERE ALL FLASCHBACK
SCENES WILL OCCUR - DAY

                        Initially the room is dark. As
                        the lights come up, we see a
                        large sitting room, with a
                        central desk and various set-

*tees and burgundy-hued wing-
back chairs scattered around the
room. There are heavy burgundy
velvet drapes framing the
windows. There is a spotlight on
James Madison, standing and
reading from a scroll of paper
with great seriousness.*

JAMES MADISON

A well-regulated militia, being necessary to the
security of a free state, the right to bear
arms, shall not be infringed.

*Thomas Jefferson enters the
room.*

THOMAS JEFFERSON

Why James, it was critical that we lay down a
framework to allow for such rights, as could only
be considered practical at the time. The political climate necessitated such, as the landscape
of our young democracy was ripe with the unknown.
As free men of sound mind and body, protection
against thieves, bandits and other realistic
uprisings was of utmost importance in maintaining
the freedom and safety of our citizens and our
country during our formative years.

*Alexander Hamilton enters the
room.*

ALEXANDER HAMILTON

... And also to serve as a reminder to the rest
of the world that our citizenry is well-armed
and prepared.

JAMES MADISON

Yes Alexander, also important at the time.
Besides the advantage of being armed, it forms a
barrier against the enterprises of ambition,
more insurmountable than any which a simple
government of any form can fall back upon. The
governments of Europe are afraid to trust the
people with arms. If they did, the people would
surely shake off the yoke of tyranny, as America
did!

THOMAS JEFFERSON

What country can preserve its liberties if their
rulers are not warned from time to time that
their people preserve the spirit of resistance.
Let them take arms.

> *George Washington enters the
> room.*

GEORGE WASHINGTON

To be prepared for war is one of the most
effectual means of preserving peace. A free
people ought not only to be armed, **BUT
DISCIPLINED**.

ALEXANDER HAMILTON

The best we can hope for concerning the people
at large is that they be properly armed. It will
ultimately be our best weapon in our efforts to
safeguard the interests of this young and noble
country.

GEORGE WASHINGTON

And that the said Constitution be never construed
to authorize Congress to infringe the just
liberty of the press, or the rights of
conscience; or to prevent the people of the
United States, who are **PEACEABLE** citizens, from
keeping their own arms.

John Adams enters the room.

JOHN ADAMS

Arms in the hands of citizens may be used at
individual discretion, in private self-defense.

THOMAS JEFFERSON

One of the strongest reasons for the people to
retain the right to keep and bear arms is, as a
last resort, to protect themselves in self-
defense and against tyranny in Government, not
to allow for indiscriminate use or to create
scenes of violence resulting in mass casualties
and injury. **Why, it defies common sense!**

JOHN ADAMS

This was not what we had in mind!

CUT TO:

I.4 INT. EARLY MORNING - JACKSON OWENS LIVING
ROOM

> *Jackson Owens is slumped over
> and asleep, snoring with his
> head on the table, surrounded
> by an empty whiskey bottle,
> his gun, his cell phone, the*

*photograph of his family and a
serious hangover. His cell
phone RINGS, waking him up out
of his drunken flirtation with
death.*

JACKIE OWENS

Hello, yes, good morning Attorney Pantovere.
Yes, I have a minute to talk with you.

MICHAEL PANTOVERE

(v.o)

Mr. Owens, FANTASTIC NEWS! The U.S. Attorney's
office has no choice but to allow your case and
the charges against Dwayne LaFollett to proceed!
Fortunately for us, their recent charges against
over 200 mostly peaceful protesters at the
January 2017 festivities at the Trump inauguration day events have left them in a difficult
position, setting an inarguable precedence for
us, as your case reveals such egregious inflammatory behavior in comparison. They forged
forward with unfounded charges that could have
put these defendants in jail for over 60 years
with no basis. LaFollett's clearly inflammatory
speech and the resulting aftermath of injury and
death are clearly more inflammatory and severe
than that which occurred during the inauguration
ceremonies. So, while they never really should
have been allowed to file those charges in the
first place, the fact that they did and were
allowed to proceed to trial, provided us with a
great advantage and precedence in allowing us to
move forward!

JACKIE OWENS

(sounding a bit dazed but pleased)

Thank you, sir! That is the best news I have
heard in a while and it gives me some hope and
encouragement that there might be some
consequences to the NRA as a result of the
inflammatory role that LaFollett played,
resulting in the murder of my family!

MICHAEL PANTOVERE

(v.o)

Sit tight, Mr. Owens! I will call you as soon as
I have any more news to share with you.

JACKIE OWENS

I will do that Attorney Pantovere and wait for
your instructions.

MICHAEL PANTOVERE

(v.o)

Mr. Owens, you don't sound well. Sir, I know you
don't have a lot of blue skies over you right
now, but will you promise me one thing?

JACKIE OWENS

If I can.

MICHAEL PANTOVERE

(v.o)

That you will not give up the good fight! Don't
let this right-winged, bull shit special
interest group of gun rights conservatives take
the wind out of your sails. You need help in
dealing with your grief and loss. Let me help
you get that. We are in a place that no one has
ever been before and I promise you that I will
give you 200% in this fight to finally take on
the NRA and we will stand tall as symbols of
hope for meaningful and permanent change to gun
laws in this country. You can do this Jackie! We
can do this together!

JACKIE OWENS

I want to believe you, Attorney Pantovere. I am
just so tired and in so much pain. I crawl out of
bed every morning and I really have nothing to
live for anymore. I watched my entire family die
before my very own eyes at an NRA Rally that they
attended because of me, at my insistence. All I
can hope for is that somehow, I can help others
who have also been affected by gun violence and
that we can bring about some type of lasting change
in gun control legislation in this country.

MICHAEL PANTOVERE

(v.o)

That's exactly what we are going to do, and we
will do it together, but I need you to get your
fight back and your will to live and to live
life with a purpose. I want you to try to
channel your pain into a resolute determination

to take a stand against LaFollett and the NRA. With your permission, I would like to share your contact information with a medical professional that I have great respect for and whom I think will be able to help you to address your pain and regain your strength and will to live.

JACKIE OWENS

(pauses for a second as he looks at his surroundings, his gun, and the empty bottle of whiskey)

Ok, maybe I need that help, thank you. I will look forward to getting more information. Thank you for your call.

Jackie HANGS up the phone.

CUT TO:

II.5. INT. - EARLY EVENING - THE HOME/DINING ROOM/ LIBRARY OF JUDGE GRACE PORTER HAVERHILL AND HER HUSBAND DR. MITCHELL HAVERHILL

A very lovely, pregnant Grace Porter Haverhill and her psychiatrist/professor husband Mitchell Haverhill are just home from work, with a television on in the background playing the Nightly News. Mitch is busy unpacking a box of books to some shelves in the library of their new home. Grace is looking in the refrigerator for something to make for dinner.

TELEVISION NEWSCASTER
(v.o.)

Tensions continue to escalate as the impending criminal trial date nears being set for the charges filed against Dwayne LaFollett, the President and speaker at the NRA rally held in Arlington earlier this year, which resulted in the death of Sally Owens and her three children, as well as thirteen others. The highly anticipated, "MOATs," or Mother of All Trials, is expected to attract huge media attention, as this will be the first trial of its magnitude against an executive in the conservative gun rights organization, with charges being filed as a result of the deadly shooting spree.

(pauses for effect)

Recent filings against other corporate executives, including the Sackler family as a result of the alleged deception and billions in profits realized from the over sensationalized marketing of Oxycontin and also the Supreme Court's ruling to allow families of the victims in the Sandy Hook shootings to file charges against the gun manufacturer, Remington Arms, lend precedence in providing very recent examples of the courts allowing for broader culpability. It seems like the law is finally allowing our legal system to speak truth to power in some of these tragic losses of innocent lives.

(pauses for effect)

Husband and former NRA member, Jackson Owens, has had an extreme change of heart regarding his loyalty to this progun organization, after watching his entire family gunned down by staunch NRA supporter, Harrison Culpepper, through a window in the hotel across the street from where the rally took place. Culpepper was quickly cornered by the FBI and local law enforcement and was killed in an exchange of gunfire shortly after. Thirteen other people were killed and there were over 200 other injuries resulting from the 6-minute shooting spree by Culpepper, using two AR-15 military style assault rifles.

GRACE PORTER HAVERHILL

(yelling from the kitchen, where she is loading the dishwasher, to Mitch)

Hey honey, turn that up, I can't hear over the running water.

Mitch turns up the volume on the television.

TELEVISION NEWSCASTER

(v.o.)

A grand jury in the Eastern District Court of the Commonwealth of Virginia, has charged LaFollett with disorderly conduct and seventeen counts of violating the federal riots act and the intent to promote and encourage a riot, as a result of the deadly progun speech made during the Arlington rally, and as a result of the NRA's high powered marketing campaigns to instill fear among our citizens, encouraging multiple gun purchases, including AR-15s and other types of military assault rifles.

(pauses for effect)

It was highly anticipated that the U.S.
Attorney's Office would not allow the charges to
be filed, but really had no choice but to allow
for these charges to move forward, because of
the precedence that they themselves set back in
2017, by charging over two hundred protesters at
President Donald Trump's inauguration day
festivities. Despite the fact that during the
first trial, the Justice Department prosecutors
admitted that there was no evidence to support
that the vast majority of the accused had
committed any violence at all! This is in sharp
contrast to the fiery and frenetic speech given
by Lafollett in a reckless and irresponsible
display of bravado, while emergency rescue teams
and medics were already attending to wounded
rally participants, as a result of the melee
that had broken out in response to the previous
speaker's rhetoric and inflammatory speech. This
is sure to be a trial like no other in modern
history, pitting gun rights activists against
gun control activists and likely, Republicans
against Democrats. Stay tuned. We'll be sure to
bring you all the latest.

> *Mitch walks over to the*
> *television and turns it off.*

MITCHELL HAVERHILL

Animals, what a bunch of animals. That poor guy
finally recognizes the error of his ways when
it's too late! I couldn't imagine losing my
wife, my kids...

> (Grabs Grace as she walks by and
> kisses her belly)

Speaking of kids, what if we have twins?

GRACE PORTER HAVERHILL

Twice the blessing!

MITCHELL HAVERHILL

Then someday, when they grow up, we could have a
lawyer and a shrink!

(laughing)

The best of both worlds!

(pauses)

Do you want to find out whether it's a boy or a
girl, or maybe both?

GRACE PORTER HAVERHILL

Hmmm... I'm not sure. I think it would be fun to
be surprised. Actually, I'd love to have twins.
Let's wait to make a decision on the other.

MITCHELL HAVERHILL

Sure, fine with me. What's for dinner? I'm tired
of unpacking already.

GRACE PORTER HAVERHILL

Something quick, soup and sandwiches? I'm tired.

(she sits down for a minute)

I have to go in early tomorrow.

(she rubs her belly)

Baby and I need our beauty sleep.

MITCHELL HAVERHILL

You get more beautiful each day!

(kisses her)

You know, there's probably a good chance you're going to be presiding over that case.

GRACE PORTER HAVERHILL

You're right. It's in our backyard and district and I'm in between cases. I guess it will depend on the case load of the other judges as well. Hey, it's fair game and I'm up for the challenge.

Grace stands up and starts to leave the room.

MITCHELL HAVERHILL

Spoken like the most famous judge in the world.

(laughing)

You certainly made a grand exit from your last case in Charlottesville. Your star is shining bright!

GRACE PORTER HAVERHILL

(laughing)

As I've heard it said before, "The price of Justice is eternal publicity."

MITCHELL HAVERHILL

If our kid's first words have anything to do
with constitutional liberties, I'm filing for a
divorce!

(laughing)

CUT TO:

I.6 INT. - OFFICE OF DWAYNE LAFOLLETT - MORNING

*Dwayne LaFollett is the
President of the NRA. A tall,
stodgy powerhouse of a man who
is having a heated discussion
with his Attorney, Leonard
Snayder.*

DWAYNE LAFOLLETT

(speaking in an agitated voice with
a reddened face)

How in the hell can they bring charges against
me? It's the stupidest thing I've heard, and it
requires time that I do not have to waste!

LEONARD SNAYDER

They can certainly try to make these charges
stick. It's a long shot, but not impossible.
Unfortunately, your buddies down at the U.S.
Attorney's Office, shot themselves in the foot
with this one.

(laughing out loud and said
somewhat under his breath)

God, I am funny!

> (pauses for effect)

While time is always an issue, I can guarantee that the gun manufacturers are going to be there rank and file to help contribute to your legal fees.

> (said with a smirk on his face)

Which is a good thing Dwayne, because at a grand an hour, I don't come cheap!

DWAYNE LAFOLLETT

I cannot believe that the speech I gave at the Arlington rally could be construed in such an offensive manner to warrant such charges as they have laid out.

LEONARD SNAYDER

Well, I've listened to it several times. It's always a matter of perception and making sure we choose a good jury will be key.

> *Getting increasingly agitated, LaFollett stands up and walks over to a side table to pour himself a glass of bourbon.*

DWAYNE LAFOLLETT

Inciting a riot! How the fuck can they try to lay that one on me? As the President of the NRA, I have every right to hold rallies and encourage our membership to support our mission!

Finishes his drink in one big swig and goes to pour himself another.

DWAYNE LAFOLLETT (CONT'D)

Want one?

LEONARD SNAYDER

Jesus, it's 9:30 in the morning Dwayne.

DWAYNE LAFOLLETT

You should see what I had for breakfast.

Finishing off his drink and setting the glass on the counter.

Hell, most of Congress is in our pocket. The courts have frequently sided in our favor with most of the recent legislation. This is just a little smoke and mirrors. This too shall pass. It always does.

LEONARD SNAYDER

True enough. But social media and the age of some of the injured and recent media attention for some of the victim's family members seem to be striking a bit of a different chord. There's been such a proliferation of mass shootings, including school shootings over the past several years, we'll just have to wait and see. The Parkland kids started a wave among younger citizens and now many of those kids are of voting age! Meanwhile, try to stay out of the spotlight, Ok? I'll be in touch as soon as I hear more.

Turns to leave.

You're not driving anywhere this afternoon, are you?

                    DWAYNE LAFOLLETT
               (yelling at the top of his lungs)

Get your Boy Scout ass out of here before I shoot you....

                              CUT TO: CLOSE ON

I.7 INT. - "THE RED ROOM" - DAY

                    George Washington is reading a
                    newspaper. John Adams is
                    pacing back and forth. Thomas
                    Jefferson, Alexander Hamilton
                    and James Madison are all
                    seated or standing in various
                    locations around the room.
                    This is the first of several
                    scenes that includes Aaron
                    Burr.

                    JOHN ADAMS

Hmmm...

               (pauses for effect)

Rather fascinating. We find ourselves looking back now upon the laws and rights that we wrote and enumerated in a manner that we structured with hopes to stand the test of time. It is now

this generation's responsibility to apply them
accordingly and realistically.

JAMES MADISON

Yes, John, I strongly stated that the
"character" of the Constitution must be tested
by the experience of the future. Laws and
institutions must go hand in hand with the
progress of the human mind. As that becomes more
developed, more enlightened, as new discoveries
are made, new truths disclosed, and manners and
opinions change with the change of
circumstances, institutions must advance also,
and keep pace with the times.

(pauses for effect)

Laws that forbid the carrying of arms, disarm
only those who are neither inclined or
determined to commit crimes. Such laws only make
things worse for the assaulted and better for
the assassins; they serve to encourage than to
prevent homicides, for an unarmed man may be
attacked with greater confidence than an armed
man. One loves to possess arms, though they hope
never to have occasion for them.

GEORGE WASHINGTON

Yes, Thomas. Well said! The rifle and the pistol
are equally indispensable. More than 99% of
them, by their silence indicate that they are in
safe and sane hands. The very atmosphere of
firearms everywhere restrains evil interference.
When firearms go, all goes, we need them every
hour. A free people should be an armed people.
It ensures against the tyranny of the
government. But as I have already stated, we

also must never lose sight of the fact that we
formed this nation to be a union of **PEACEABLE**
people. Where the reasoning of our words and the
honesty of our intentions would triumph over
tyranny and lawlessness.

THOMAS JEFFERSON

The tree of **LIBERTY** must be refreshed from time
to time with the blood of patriots and tyrants.
It is its natural manure.

ALEXANDER HAMILTON

It has been frequently remarked that it seems to
have been reserved to the people of this
country, by their conduct and example, to decide
the important question, whether societies of men
are really capable or not of establishing good
government from reflection and choice, or
whether they are forever destined to depend for
their political constitutions on accident and
FORCE.

GEORGE WASHINGTON

That seems to be the predicament we witness
here. Why, when the Second Amendment was
ratified in 1791, there was certainly a fair
measure of gun control. Regulation was certainly
intact, stating who could own firearms.

(pauses for effect)

Many states had laws prohibiting various
citizens from possessing firearms. States also
conducted gun censuses. The right to gun
ownership was not absolute! The formation of
state militias provided our citizens with both a

defense against external attack and defense against the potential suppression by a tyrannical, federal government. However ineffective the militias were, that was their intended purpose. At the time of the amendment's enforcement, state laws limited gun ownership to those between the ages of 18 and 45 who were able to serve in the militia.

AARON BURR

And yet, I have also heard it said that the phrase gun control refers to who is the better shot!

(chuckling to himself and giving an exaggerated wink to his nemesis, Alexander Hamilton.)

ALEXANDER HAMILTON

To my previous point, Machiavelli so aptly stated that, "You must understand, therefore, that there are two ways of fighting: by law or by force. The first way is natural to men, and the second to beasts. But as the first way often proves inadequate one must have recourse to the second."

JOHN ADAMS

(appearing to be lost in thought)

So shall our future generations choose the former...

(pauses for effect)

Or the latter? Let us pray for men over beasts good gentlemen, let us pray...

CUT TO:

ACT II

JUSTIFICATION

II.1 INT. - COURTROOM - MORNING

> *There are throngs of protesters gathered outside the courtroom representing both sides of the argument, gun rights and gun control advocates. There is mass confusion and shouting, with each side holding banners espousing their views.*

BAILIFF

All rise. The Honorable Grace Porter Haverhill is now presiding.

> *Grace enters the courtroom from her chambers, takes her seat, and POUNDS the gavel.*

GRACE PORTER HAVERHILL

Be seated please. Today we are gathered to hear the opening arguments in The Eastern District Court of the Commonwealth of Virginia v. Dwayne LaFollett. Mr. LaFollett has been charged with disorderly conduct, as well as seventeen counts of violating the federal riots act and the intent to promote and encourage a riot as a result of the May 5, 2018 NRA rally here in Arlington. A total of seventeen people were killed and 203 others injured as a result of the shooting spree carried out by Harrison Culpepper from two windows in a room on the top floor of the hotel across the street. These charges have been filed By Mr. Jackson Owens, whose wife and three children were killed as a result of this mass shooting. Mr. Pantovere, Mr. Snayder, are you ready to proceed with opening arguments?

> *Both attorneys stand in unison. Michael Pantovere, the attorney for the prosecution, is a tall, serious, outspoken advocate for our Constitution and the Bill of Rights. Leonard Snayder, the crafty-looking attorney for the defense, has an "anything goes" reputation for trying to win cases using questionable means.*

MICHAEL PANTOVERE/LEONARD SNAYDER

We are, your Honor!

GRACE PORTER HAVERHILL

Very well then, Mr. Pantovere, proceed please.

MICHAEL PANTOVERE

Ladies and gentlemen of the jury, family members who lost loved ones and are seated here witnessing these proceedings today, I stand here before you as an officer of the court and on behalf of Jackson Owens, in an effort to hold accountable the man whose inflammatory speech triggered one of the worst mass shootings in the history of this country.

(pauses for effect)

You know what really gets me? All of the senators who tirelessly and incessantly send their thoughts and prayers and yes, that is all they send. Pretty words and feigned sentiments serving as a cloak for inaction and the preservation of self-interests. No action...just thoughts and prayers.

(pauses for effect)

Why even words and judgements will never bring their loved ones back, but words and judgements can perhaps shape the future so that repeat occurrences of similar types of events are less likely to occur as a result of changes in behavior and as a result of meaningful gun control legislation. Let me stress from the outset that no one hear is even remotely suggesting that the answer is to repeal the Second Amendment! Gun rights advocates are always quick to assume that is the end goal. It is not! This is a court of law not Congress! We are here today in an effort to hold Mr. LaFollett accountable for an openly hostile expression of speech that encouraged and incited riotous behavior in a crowd of a thousand.

(pauses for effect)

I'm sure you have all seen this footage on the local and world news many times over the past several months but as we get started in presenting our evidence, we submit to the court as Exhibit A, the tape of Mr. LaFollett's speech

of May 5, 2018 at the NRA rally here in
Arlington. Bailiff please roll the tape.

> *The Bailiff plays the tape for*
> *the jury and courtroom, as*
> *Harrison Culpepper begins his*
> *shooting spree into the crowd*
> *gathered for the Arlington NRA*
> *rally. The tape ends and there*
> *is an uncomfortable look on*
> *the jurors' faces.*

MICHAEL PANTOVERE (CONT'D)

Seventeen people murdered IN COLD BLOOD and 203
others injured as a result of this inflammatory
and violence inducing speech!

LEONARD SNAYDER

Objection, your Honor! Counsel is convicting my
client before we even get started here!

GRACE PORTER HAVERHILL

Sustained! Mr. Pantovere watch your wording,
please!

MICHAEL PANTOVERE

Of course, your Honor! I just don't understand
how an educated man and the elected leader of an
organization could be as short-sighted as to
think that it was a good idea to further rile up
an already emotionally inflamed crowd of a
thousand, where tensions were already running
high and violence was breaking out. We are
asking that the defendant be charged with the

maximum criminal penalties available and other
relief that the Court deems necessary and just.
The Eastern District Court of the Commonwealth
of Virginia intends to prove Mr. LaFollett's
guilt beyond a reasonable doubt.

> *Pantovere takes his seat and*
> *Attorney Snayder stands and*
> *starts to address the jury and*
> *courtroom.*

LEONARD SNAYDER

Ladies and gentlemen of the jury, witnesses here
in the courtroom today, it is hard for me to
believe that we gather here this morning with
the need to defend the district's baseless
effort to hold my client, Dwayne LaFollett,
accountable for the act of a deranged gunman,
namely Harrison Culpepper, who met his demise
when confronted by the Arlington police in an
exchange of gunfire at the hotel. My client is
an innocent man! He is the President of the
prestigious National Rifle Association and a
defender of our Second Amendment rights. He has
every right to give a passionate speech at a
gathering of his supporters. Not only is that in
keeping with his Second Amendment rights, it's
also in keeping with his First Amendment rights,
the right to free speech and to peaceful
assembly.

(pauses for effect)

Repealing and/or curtailing the scope of the
Second Amendment has become the cry of scores of
liberal, left wing snowflakes that have a very
poor understanding of the truth, of the facts.
If you really listened to the words my client

spoke during the speech we just viewed, what he
was speaking, was quite simply, the truth. Gun
sales actually do increase after mass shootings.
NRA memberships actually do continue to
increase. Why, the NRA broke its fundraising
record in March 2018, realizing $2.4 Million in
donations, which is the most money it has raised
in a single month since 2003, despite the fact
that this herculean effort directly proceeded
the February 2018 Parkland school shooting!

                    MICHAEL PANTOVERE

Your Honor, I just have to interject here. Since
the Parkland shooting, overall support for
stricter gun regulation has increased across the
board but remains a highly partisan issue.

                    LEONARD SNAYDER

Well, my statistics tell a different story!
There have been large public shows of support
against additional gun control legislation at
state houses across the country. I certainly
think it can be said that there are too many
crazy people out there whose gun ownership
rights should be curtailed or denied, but that
really is the responsibility of the medical
community and to some extent, law enforcement.

                 (pauses for effect)

I just can't believe that the U.S. Attorney's
office allowed for these charges to be filed. I
intend to prove that my client, Dwayne
LaFollett, is innocent of all charges being
brought against him here today by the Eastern
District Court of The Commonwealth of Virginia.

(pauses for effect)

It was once said, "The Republican form of government is the highest form of government but because of this it requires the highest type of human nature - a type nowhere at present existing." Guns play a critical role in safeguarding our personal liberties, namely the Second Amendment. I thank you, the jury for your service. I have nothing further.

> *Snayder takes his seat, and Attorney Pantovere stands to again address the court.*

MICHAEL PANTOVERE

Your Honor, I would like to address a comment just made by Attorney Snayder, in making sure that the jury and everyone else gathered here today understands exactly why the U.S. Attorney's Office had no choice but to allow for these charges to be filed. Since you presided over that case, your Honor, those reasons are in your not too distant memory.

(pauses for effect)

The U.S. District Attorney's office allowed for charges to be brought against over two hundred protesters as a result of activities during the 2017 Inauguration of Donald Trump, where no one was killed, six police officers were hospitalized and there was only $100,000 in property damage realized. A drop in the bucket when compared to the mass carnage that occurred at the recent NRA rally in Arlington! The Justice Department's prosecutors blatantly and openly conceded that there was absolutely NO evidence to support that the majority of those arrested and charged during the inauguration ceremonies had committed any violence whatsoever! The charges were overreaching and sensationalized and were clearly of a political nature, in an effort to intimidate our citizens against speaking out against the newly elected administration. They even tried to charge the group with a felony count of inciting a riot, for which you issued a judgment of acquittal up front, much to the dismay of the Justice Department. Collectively, these charges could have resulted in these innocent defendants facing jail time of over sixty years each.

(pauses for effect)

I'm sure you recall, the first six protesters were found innocent of all charges but only after turning their lives upside down, resulting in many of them having to quit their jobs and temporarily relocate to the D.C. area to satisfy the overzealous prosecutorial demands and suffer massive legal fees to defend their First Amendment rights! Two of the arrested were actually street medics, carrying medical supplies and yet the charges were allowed to stick! Ultimately all of the remaining charges ended up being dropped for all protesters, except for roughly the 10% who actually did commit various illegal activities and who got charged and sentenced accordingly.

(pauses for effect)

Interestingly enough, Michael Loadenthal, a professor at Miami University, who himself was one of the "J20" defendants, recently wrote a paper discussing "the felonization and

riotization of protests," under the Trump
administration.

(pauses for effect)

So, you see, ladies and gentlemen of the jury
and other witnesses here in court today, if the
U.S. Attorney's office HADN'T allowed these
charges to be filed, they would have been
legitimately able to be labeled HYPOCRITES! Mr.
LaFollett's speech was clearly inflammatory and
inappropriate fodder to further whip up a crowd
where tensions were high, and the police were
struggling to break up the pandemonium that was
ensuing as a result. I'm sure many of you recall
the Federal Assault Weapons Ban that was in
effect in the US from 1994 - 2004. Various
studies conclude that gun massacres fell 37%
during the ban and increased by 183% in the ten
years after it lapsed. There are some deviations
regarding those percentages, but you still have
to wonder if many of these mass shootings that
have taken place since 2004 might not have been
as deadly, if military assault weapons were
banned or more difficult to obtain.

(pauses for effect)

Congress has since refused to pass any similar
types of sweeping regulations and you just have
to wonder if it isn't because of the lobbying
efforts of Mr. LaFollett and his NRA that
contributed $54 million during the 2016
election, to help secure Republican control of
the White House and Congress, including $30.3
million to help elect President Trump.

(pauses for effect)

Unfortunately, we now find ourselves living in an alternate reality, with an administration that has no regard for speaking the truth and for spinning "alternative facts" as the truth whenever necessary. Well let me tell you one thing, ladies and gentlemen, I am convinced now more than ever that **WORDS MATTER**! It is my sincere hope that in allowing for this unprecedented case to move forward, as we witness here today in this court of law, that Mr. LaFollett will be held accountable for his words and the destruction and immediate lawless action that followed.

LEONARD SNAYDER

Objection! Your Honor, let me respond to Mr. Pantovere's suggestion that Congress is "in the pocket" of the NRA. The truth of the matter is that the NRA's contributions make up a very small proportion of lobbyist money received. Why, the NRA doesn't even make the "top 50." I felt the need to make that clarification, your Honor.

GRACE PORTER HAVERHILL

Sustained! Thank you, Mr. Snayder for providing that clarification!

MICHAEL PANTOVERE

As the First Amendment does NOT provide absolute immunity for all forms of speech, it can also be said that the Second Amendment does NOT provide absolute immunity for all uses of firearms. So here is the critical difference,

(pauses for effect)

the Bill of Rights is indeed meant to protect one's rights, but it does not confer the capacity to infringe on the rights of others! Let me just restate my previous comment, **WORDS MATTER!** I hope that these proceedings might result in each and every one of us starting to give thoughtful consideration to the words we speak as you never have the opportunity to take them back once you speak them and the damage can be irreparable. Since this shooting and several other recent mass shootings, states have started to take a stand and pass meaningful gun control legislation. Mr. Owens cannot get his family back, so all he can hope for is that the guilty are held accountable and that ongoing gun control legislation will be enforced.

(pauses for effect)

In preparing for this case, I read what I found to be a very interesting and disturbing article by Max Fisher and Josh Keller in the NY Times, in November of 2017, which tried to explain and contrast the mass shootings in the United States to other countries. Its conclusion was that, "the difference is culture. The United States is one of only three countries, along with Mexico and Guatemala, that begin with the opposite assumption: that people have an inherent right to own guns. After Britain had a mass shooting in 1987, the country instituted strict gun control laws. So did Australia after a 1996 shooting. [Most recently, New Zealand Prime Minister, Jacinda Ardern announced a ban on assault rifles within a week of two mass shootings that left 50 people dead.] But the United States has repeatedly faced the same calculus and determined that relatively unregulated gun ownership is worth the cost to society."

(pauses for effect)

Dan Hodges, a British journalist, further
commented in a Twitter post referring to the
Sandy Hook mass shooting that killed 20
children, by stating, "In retrospect Sandy Hook
marked the end of the US gun control debate.
Once America decided killing children was
bearable, it was over."

(pauses for effect)

Unfortunately, that is the prevailing sentiment
of our elected officials, lobbyists and gun
rights organizations that bring us to the case
at hand. All we get are thoughts and prayers! I
have nothing further your Honor!

Pantovere takes his seat.

GRACE PORTER HAVERHILL

That will conclude our session for the day.
Court is adjourned until Monday.

POUNDING the gavel.

BAILIFF

All rise....

*Grace stands and exits the
courtroom to her chambers. The
jurors file out of the
courtroom and the attorneys
gather their paperwork and
close their briefcases as they
stand and walk out of the
courtroom.*

II.2 INT. "THE RED ROOM" - DAY

> *George Washington is reading a newspaper. John Adams is pacing back and forth. Thomas Jefferson, Alexander Hamilton, James Madison, and Aaron Burr are all seated or standing at various locations around the room.*

JAMES MADISON

(Pacing back and forth slowly and rubbing his forehead as to encourage a suitable response to these proceedings they witness)

Why gentlemen, I must say I am a bit perplexed right now, as we listen to these courtroom proceedings and what seems to have become commonplace, in these occurrences of mass slaughterings of our citizenry, by advanced automations in weaponry. Our Constitution plainly gives Congress the authority to amend the Bill of Rights. Furthermore, the Bill of Rights stands to protect against a usurpation of power by the federal government, but it does not limit a state's right to pass intelligent legislation regarding the right to keep and bear arms.

GEORGE WASHINGTON

Those are the facts James; those were our intentions!

JOHN ADAMS

Why, those that are honored to serve in our
Congress are elected of, by and for the people!
Congress is there to uphold our Constitution and
represent their respective constituencies. How
has it come to pass that they have not enacted
legislation to ensure **DOMESTIC TRANQUILITY**? It
is their responsibility as a servant to their
constituents.

THOMAS JEFFERSON

Whenever a man has cast a longing eye on
offices, a rottenness begins in his conduct.

(pauses for effect)

If the present Congress errs in too much
talking, how can it be otherwise in a body to
which the people send a bunch of lawyers, whose
trade it is to question everything, yield
nothing, and talk by the hour? That lawyers
should do business together ought not to be
expected.

JAMES MADISON

Why words two and three of the Second Amendment
are "well" and "regulated," it assumes, no
requires that provisions be made for monitoring
and enforcing laws that will keep order both in
times of peace and of war. We did not intend for
the Second Amendment to serve as a safeguard for
such powerful and destructive weaponry to be
made available for ownership by all citizenry.
Why, that defies logic! It defies common sense!
Owning a musket or pistol or two to protect
one's home and family and to hunt for food to
feed oneself and their family is surely a natural

right! During our nascent years in forming this country, it was also a necessity to be able to defend oneself and the states against tyranny.

JOHN ADAMS

A true statement, James! We had just defended this burgeoning young nation from an invasion of Redcoats trying to impose their laws and taxes upon us and keep us under their onerous control.

GEORGE WASHINGTON

Quite right, man! Citizen soldiers rose up right alongside my troops to help defend our freedom and force the Redcoats to retreat.

ALEXANDER HAMILTON

Why George, as our first commander-in-chief during The Revolutionary War, starting with The Siege of Boston, two decisive victories at Trenton and Princeton, and in the forming of a staunch allegiance with the French and the penultimate siege at Yorktown, your leadership was the ray of hope and courage our troops needed to stay the course and earn our freedom.

GEORGE WASHINGTON

Oh Alexander, let us not forget that there were many defeats along the way until victory was realized. The might and strength of our adversary certainly had the cards stacked against us. It was not an even playing field. Our victory was a standing miracle. Our citizenry should focus on giving thanks and praise for the freedoms they enjoy, for every man and their lineage helped to achieve it and move forward to this day.

THOMAS JEFFERSON

Prudence, indeed, will dictate that governments long established should not be changed for light and transient causes; and accordingly all experience hath shown that mankind are more disposed to suffer, while evils are sufferable, than to right themselves by abolishing the forms to which they are accustomed.

(pauses for effect)

But when a long train of abuses and usurpations, pursuing invariably the same object, evinces a design to reduce them under absolute despotism, it is their right, it is their duty, to throw off such a government, and to provide new guards for their future security.

JAMES MADISON

There are more instances of the abridgment of the freedom of the people by gradual and silent encroachments of those in power than by violent and sudden usurpations.

THOMAS JEFFERSON

And yet, it sounds like these modern-day politicians are being influenced by those with special interests who are lining their pockets with gold, in order to be in favor and advance their causes?

GEORGE WASHINGTON

Few men have virtue to withstand the highest bidder.

JOHN ADAMS

Honest and generous spirits will disdain to deceive the people; and if the public service is willfully rendered burdensome, they will really be averse to be in it; but hypocrites enough will be found, who will pretend to be also loth to serve, and feign a reluctant consent for the public good, while they mean to plunder in every way they can conceal, betraying those who conveyed the right to serve upon them.

JAMES MADISON

Why we formed a representative democracy to protect against undue influence by factions or special interest groups.

AARON BURR

Why Alexander, perhaps we should call this turn of events "The Hamiltonian Effect?" You and your "corrupt squadron," seemed to reap great financial benefits engaging in financial speculation while holding office. In private, calling our Constitution, "a shilly shally thing!"

ALEXANDER HAMILTON

The diversity in the faculties of men, from which the rights of property originate, is... an insuperable obstacle to a uniformity of interests. The protection of these faculties is

the first object of government. From the
protection of different and unequal faculties of
acquiring property the possession of different
degrees and kinds of property immediately
results; and from the influence of those on the
sentiments and views of the respective
proprietors, ensues a division of the society
into two different interests and parties.

THOMAS JEFFERSON

Why, Alexander. I agree with you that there is a
natural aristocracy among men. The grounds are
virtue and talents... There is also an
artificial aristocracy founded on wealth and
birth, without either virtue or talents... Are
you watching these proceedings with blinders on,
Alexander? This LaFollett fellow cannot be
allowed to use the guise of the law to cloak his
intentions for furthering his special interests
at the risk of the safety of the citizenry of
our country!

ALEXANDER HAMILTON

(said with great pomposity)

A good wit will make use of anything. I will
turn diseases to commodity. Industry is
industry, my dear Thomas, your approval is not a
prerequisite for entertaining unpopular views.

AARON BURR

How quickly nature falls into revolt when gold
becomes her object.

THOMAS JEFFERSON

Agriculture, manufactures, commerce and navigation, the four pillars of our prosperity, are the most thriving when left to individual enterprise.

(pauses for effect)

I know my own principles to be pure, and therefore am not ashamed of them. On the contrary, I wish them known, and therefore willingly express them to everyone. They are the same I have acted on from the year 1775 to this day, and are the same, I am sure, with those of the great body of the American people.

(pauses for effect)

I have the consolation of having added nothing to my private fortune during my public service, and of retiring with hands as clean as they are empty. The whole act of government consists in the art of being honest.

CUT TO:

II.3 INT. - EARLY EVENING - THE HOME/OFFICE/LIBRARY OF JUDGE GRACE PORTER HAVERHILL AND HER HUSBAND DR. MITCHELL HAVERHILL

Grace is sitting at her desk doing some research on her laptop as Mitch enters the room and hands her a cup of tea.

MITCHELL HAVERHILL

So, how was your first day of the trial?

GRACE PORTER HAVERHILL

Well, off to a good start. Nothing unexpected today.

MITCHELL HAVERHILL

I really hope that when all is said and done that meaningful gun control legislation is finally put on the table and on the floor of Congress. I have to believe that a middle ground can be found. You always hear the extremists on both sides shouting about civil liberties. Both sides frequently take an "absolutist" position.

GRACE PORTER HAVERHILL

Right, each side always embraces the viewpoint that what they like is constitutional and what they don't like is unconstitutional.

CUT TO:

II.4 THE RED ROOM - SAME TIME

Alexander Hamilton is intently watching and listening to the conversation between Grace and Mitch.

ALEXANDER HAMILTON

So numerous indeed and so powerful are the causes, which serve to give a false bias to the judgment, that we upon many occasions, see wise and good men on the wrong as well as on the right side of questions, of the first magnitude to society.

(pauses for effect)

This circumstance, if duly attended to, would
furnish a lesson of moderation to those, who are
ever so much persuaded of their being in the
right, in any controversy. And a further reason
for caution, in this respect, might be drawn
from the reflection, that we are not always
sure, that those who advocate the truth are
influenced by purer principles than their
antagonists.

(pauses for effect)

Ambition, avarice, personal animosity, party
opposition, and many other motives, not more
laudable than these, are apt to operate as well
upon those who support as upon those who oppose
the right side of a question. Were there not
even these inducements to moderation, nothing
could be more ill-judged than that intolerant
spirit, which has, at all times, characterized
political parties.

CUT TO:

II.5 INT. - EARLY EVENING - THE
HOME/OFFICE/LIBRARY OF JUDGE GRACE PORTER
HAVERHILL AND HER HUSBAND DR. MITCHELL HAVERHILL
- SAME TIME

MITCHELL HAVERHILL

The evolution and destructive nature of guns
have, I am sure, far surpassed what our founding
fathers ever could have imagined. Their creation
of a "living document," should allow for some
adjustments every two hundred years or so, don't
you agree?

48

GRACE PORTER HAVERHILL

Absolutely! The destructiveness of firearms has
definitely changed, which is why the
Constitution has a mechanism for amendments.

(pauses for effect)

After today's opening arguments, I thought it
would be a good idea to make sure I am up to
speed on some current gun violence statistics
and I must say some of these findings are both
surprising and disturbing. Listen to this: the
firearm death toll between 1968-2011 in the U.S.
was greater than all wars we have ever fought,
totaling 1.4 Million firearm deaths during that
period versus 1.2 Million U.S. Deaths in every
conflict from the War of Independence to Iraq!
There are over 390 million guns in the U.S.,
which is the highest rate of per capita firearm
ownership in the world, with 3% of Americans
owning 133 million firearms. Owning more than
forty guns is fairly common in the U.S., with an
estimated 7.7 Million "super owners." More than
half of U.S. gun homicides happened in just 127
cities and towns, which together have less than
a quarter of the nation's population.

MITCHELL HAVERHILL

Yeah, it's no secret that cities like Chicago,
Detroit, and New Orleans have a disproportionate
share of gun violence. The poorest neighborhoods
are the most vulnerable.

GRACE PORTER HAVERHILL

In 2018, 2019 and 2020, there were 340, 417 and
611 mass shootings respectively. USA Today
recently stated that a mass shooting takes place

roughly every two weeks. Americans are more likely to die from firearms than many other leading causes of death combined.

MITCHELL HAVERHILL

You're never going to find a gun in this peace-loving household again! I appreciate your turning in your pistol to the local police. I guess pregnancy changed your position on this issue and I am grateful!

GRACE PORTER HAVERHILL

I agree that the framers could have never envisioned AR-15 or AK-47 assault weapons. While the Supreme Court has typically refused to hear the majority of gun control cases brought before it. The rulings in both Heller and McDonald uphold the right to bear arms as an individual right but does not preclude all regulations, including, "particularly dangerous and unusual weapons." You know, I'm not sure that Daddy would have agreed with the initial decision handed down for Heller and subsequently McDonald. For the 125 years prior to the Heller ruling, the Court had always ruled that the Second Amendment did not bar the limiting or removal of guns owned by individuals and typically flipped it back to the states.

(pauses for effect)

Erin N. Griswold, former Dean of Harvard Law School, commented, "Never in history has a federal court invalidated a law regulating the private ownership of firearms on Second Amendment grounds. Indeed, that the Second Amendment poses no barrier to strong gun laws is

perhaps the most well settled proposition in
American constitutional law." Then the McDonald
ruling followed. Hopefully these two rulings
will not backfire, resulting in states re-
evaluating and scaling back important gun
control laws. I think that if my Father were
still alive in 2008, he would have joined RBG,
Souter, Stevens, and Breyer in dissenting on
Heller, despite his conservative leaning voting
history!

(pauses for effect)

Back in 1991, former Chief Justice Burger said
that the Second Amendment, "has been the subject
of one of the greatest pieces of fraud, on the
American public by special interest groups that
I have ever seen in my lifetime," and he was a
conservative!

MITCHELL HAVERHILL

Right, I really think Congress should pass
another Assault Rifle ban like they did from
1994-2004.

GRACE PORTER HAVERHILL

(staring at her laptop screen)

The statistics I read say that from 1984 to
1994, the ten year period prior to the ban,
there were a total of 19 incidents and 155
deaths, from 1994 to 2004, during the ban, there
were 12 incidents and 89 deaths, from 2004-2014,
in the ten year period after the ban expired,
there were 34 incidents and 302 deaths, which is
clearly a significant increase! The ban was

clearly effective in reducing the carnage of mass shootings!

MITCHELL HAVERHILL

It's always interesting how each side seems to conveniently quote statistics favorable to their side of the argument! Every poll I have read says that the vast majority of Americans are overwhelmingly in favor of common-sense gun control legislation. A majority of Americans support stricter gun laws, universal background checks and banning the sale of assault weapons, so why is Congress refusing to act?

GRACE PORTER HAVERHILL

I guess you need to ask Congress. I have no clue and I'm still a Republican. The majority of Americans support mandatory waiting periods for gun purchases and 53% approve of high capacity magazine bans. Over 70% of Americans support requiring a license to purchase a gun.

(pauses for effect)

Switzerland and Finland require gun owners to acquire licenses and pass background checks that include mental and criminal records among other restrictions and requirements.

MITCHELL HAVERHILL

Someday, I hope I will convince you to officially embrace the democratic platform, but you have become much more open to listening to my point of view. I guess marriage agrees with you.

52

>He walks over to her at her
>desk and helps her up from the
>chair.

MITCHELL HAVERHILL (CONT'D)

Come on baby mama, it's time to get some shut
eye. You have another long day in front of you
tomorrow!

GRACE PORTER HAVERHILL

True enough. Let's call it a day.

>They walk out of the room
>together and turn off the
>lights.

CUT TO:

II.6 INT. - COURTROOM - MORNING

>There are throngs of
>protesters gathered outside
>the courtroom representing
>both sides of the argument,
>gun rights and gun control
>advocates. There is mass
>confusion and shouting, with
>each side holding banners
>espousing their views.

BAILIFF

All rise. The Honorable Grace Porter Haverhill
is now presiding.

Grace enters the courtroom from her chambers, takes her seat, and POUNDS the gavel.

GRACE PORTER HAVERHILL

Be seated please. Today we are gathered to hear ongoing arguments in The Eastern District Court of The Commonwealth of Virginia v. Dwayne LaFollett. Mr. LaFollett has been charged with disorderly conduct and seventeen counts of violating the federal riots act, as well as promoting and encouraging a riot as a result of the May 5, 2018 NRA rally here in Arlington. Mr. Pantovere, Mr. Snayder, are you ready to get started?

Both Attorneys stand and speak in unison.

MICHAEL PANTOVERE/LEONARD SNAYDER

We are, your Honor!

GRACE PORTER HAVERHILL

Very well, Mr. Pantovere, proceed please.

MICHAEL PANTOVERE

Thank you, your Honor. We are here today to continue in presenting the evidence against Mr. LaFollett as a result of the mass shooting that occurred at the May 5, 2018 NRA rally. My first witness is Chief of Police, Timothy Miller, who was in charge of the Arlington Police response for the event on that day. Please take the stand Chief Miller.

> *Timothy Miller walks up to the stand and takes a seat in the witness chair as the Bailiff approaches with the Bible.*

BAILIFF

Please place your right hand on the bible and repeat after me, I, Timothy Miller, swear to tell the whole truth and nothing but the truth, so help me God.

> *Chief Miller repeats the vow and takes a seat as Attorney Pantovere approaches the stand.*

MICHAEL PANTOVERE

Chief Miller, you were present and in charge of security for the NRA rally here in Arlington, VA on May 5, 2018, correct sir?

TIMOTHY MILLER

That is correct.

MICHAEL PANTOVERE

What time did you arrive at the rally site and please explain the circumstances you witnessed upon arrival.

TIMOTHY MILLER

We arrived at 12:00PM, approximately two hours in advance of the event to make sure that we had the necessary barricades in place and to give my

team enough time to get well positioned so that
we could manage the anticipated crowd.

MICHAEL PANTOVERE

What size crowd were you anticipating and what
size did the crowd end up being? Also, please
briefly size up your assessment regarding the
demeanor and volatility of the crowd.

TIMOTHY MILLER

We were expecting anywhere from 800-1,000 total
attendees or more, to include both NRA
members/supporters and gun control activists.
There were probably about 100 attendees already
there at 12:00PM and the number grew to over
1,000 by the time the rally started at 2:00PM. I
would estimate that there were more NRA members
there than gun control activists maybe a 70-30
breakdown. The gun control activists were
definitely outnumbered and had plenty of signs
and were chanting various gun control slogans.
Initially, the crowd on both sides seemed well
behaved.

MICHAEL PANTOVERE

Ok, so to recap, the crowd turned out to be
about the size you had anticipated, or maybe a
bit more. There were roughly two NRA supporters
for every one gun control advocate and the crowd
was well behaved in the beginning. Is that
correct?

TIMOTHY MILLER

Yes, that is correct.

MICHAEL PANTOVERE

So, since this was an NRA rally, all of the
speakers were progun/NRA members, correct?

TIMOTHY MILLER

Correct.

MICHAEL PANTOVERE

Ok, so the first speaker got started at around
2:00PM and how long did that last and how many
speakers were there in total, prior to Mr.
LaFollett taking the stage?

TIMOTHY MILLER

Yes, the first speaker started right around
2:00PM and his speech lasted for about 15
minutes. There were two other speakers after the
first and their speeches also both lasted about
15 minutes. It was during the third speaker's
talk that things started to get contentious.

MICHAEL PANTOVERE

Ok, so at about 2:30PM that afternoon the third
speaker started to incense the crowd of gun
control advocates? What was said to create the
tensions?

TIMOTHY MILLER

Yes, at about 2:30PM the third speaker started
to make reference to the Parkland school
shooting survivors which really seemed to anger
many in the crowd.

MICHAEL PANTOVERE

I see, exactly what did the speaker say about
the Parkland students that angered the crowd?

TIMOTHY MILLER

He said they were, "whiny little bitches,
looking for their 15 minutes of fame." He called
them the "fake news media darlings." He quoted
the NRA President as saying, "Crying white
mothers are ratings gold." They blamed the FBI,
local law enforcement and mental health
practitioners and called for arming teachers.
Violence started breaking out and gun control
activists started charging at some NRA members.

MICHAEL PANTOVERE

Hmmm... whiny little bitches looking for their
15 minutes of fame? What an awful thing to say
about a student body who had just buried
seventeen of their own! How long did it take for
the violence to start getting out of hand?

TIMOTHY MILLER

Not long. Maybe 5 minutes. Keep in mind that the
gun control advocates were outnumbered two to
one.

MICHAEL PANTOVERE

How were the NRA members threatening these gun
control advocates at this point?

TIMOTHY MILLER

It was heavy physical contact. In numerous
instances, NRA members were collectively
restraining gun control advocates and pummeling
them with their fists and kicking them in the
ribs. It got nasty fast, but at first, it seemed
like we had the situation under control and had
enough of the force on the ground to break up
the fights and get those injured in ambulances
and on their way to get medical help.

MICHAEL PANTOVERE

So, at this point, how many gun control
advocates would you estimate were injured badly
enough to require medical attention?

TIMOTHY MILLER

Maybe 10 or so, maybe 15.

MICHAEL PANTOVERE

Ok, so there were roughly 300 gun control
advocates there and within 5-10 minutes, 10-15
of them were injured enough to require medical
attention, correct?

TIMOTHY MILLER

Correct!

MICHAEL PANTOVERE

So, the NRA speakers were getting the crowd
pumped up for President Dwayne LaFollett's
speech which evidently was scheduled to start
around 2:45PM that afternoon, correct?

TIMOTHY MILLER

Correct!

MICHAEL PANTOVERE

Can you tell me what happened when the President
of the NRA, Dwayne LaFollett, took the stage?

TIMOTHY MILLER

Certainly, for the first five minutes or so,
things quieted down a bit, which was helpful to
us on the ground. We were able to get those that
needed medical help off to area hospitals and
try to regain control of the situation.

MICHAEL PANTOVERE

Thank you. Chief Miller, after 30 years on the
police force, do you think that there is any way
that when Dwayne LaFollett took the stage, that
he could have been unaware that there had been
violence occurring? To the extent that it
required medical attention and victims being
transported off of the premises in ambulances
with sirens blaring?

LEONARD SNAYDER

Objection! Calls for speculation, your Honor!

MICHAEL PANTOVERE

Your Honor, I disagree, 10-15 injured people on
the ground would necessitate ambulances and
other emergency medical technicians to attend to
their needs. This was not occurring in a vacuum!

GRACE PORTER HAVERHILL

Overruled, Mr. Snayder. Please answer the
question Chief Miller.

TIMOTHY MILLER

No, your Honor. There were ambulance sirens and
the typical commotion on the ground when
emergency medical support is required. Unless
Mr. LaFollett was deaf and blind, there is no
way that he could not have seen what was
transpiring.

MICHAEL PANTOVERE

Thank you, Chief Miller. Ok, so you said after
Dwayne LaFollett took the stage, there was a
brief respite and things calmed down for a few
minutes. What happened next?

TIMOTHY MILLER

Well, it got to the point about 8-10 minutes
into Mr. LaFollett's speech, when he started
talking about GUNS, GUNS, GUNS! In assessing the
situation on the ground, I was just starting to
walk up to the stage to ask Mr. Lafollett to
either dial down his rhetoric or cut his speech
short and that's when all hell broke loose!

MICHAEL PANTOVERE

And what happened next, Chief Miller?

TIMOTHY MILLER

Well, several skirmishes started to break out
with NRA members. We were responding to those

injuries when the shots started to ring out from
the top floor of a building across the way,
which ended up being the hotel across the
street. Clearly sir, there was no way we could
have ever been prepared for the nightmare that
was unfolding. The entire crowd, both NRA
members/supporters and gun control advocates
were being assaulted from above by semi-
automatic gunfire. By the time all was said and
done, seventeen people, including both NRA
members and gun control advocates were murdered
and over 200 were injured. I have never seen
anything like it in my entire 30 years on the
force and I hope to God, I never will again!

                    MICHAEL PANTOVERE

Thank you, Chief. I have nothing further.

                 GRACE PORTER HAVERHILL

Ready to cross, Mr. Snayder?

                    LEONARD SNAYDER

Yes, your Honor.

                 GRACE PORTER HAVERHILL

Proceed!

                    LEONARD SNAYDER

Chief Miller, at any time, did any of the NRA
speakers prior to Dwayne LaFollett, urge or
instruct attending NRA members or supporters to
retaliate upon gun control advocates in
attendance the afternoon of May 5, 2018?

TIMOTHY MILLER

No sir.

LEONARD SNAYDER

Chief Miller, at any time, did Dwayne LaFollett
urge or instruct attending NRA members or
supporters to retaliate upon gun control
advocates in attendance the afternoon of May 5,
2018?

TIMOTHY MILLER

No sir.

LEONARD SNAYDER

You previously stated that you were about to go
up to the stage and ask Mr. Lafollett to dial
down his rhetoric or cut his speech short, is
that correct, Chief Miller?

TIMOTHY MILLER

Yes, that is correct.

LEONARD SNAYDER

But you never actually did make that request,
did you?

TIMOTHY MILLER

No, I wasn't able to.

LEONARD SNAYDER

I have nothing further, your Honor.

GRACE PORTER HAVERHILL

Thank you, Chief Miller. You may step down.

> *Chief Miller exits the stand
> and Leonard Snayder takes his
> seat. Michael Pantovere rises
> to call his next witness.*

MICHAEL PANTOVERE

My next witness is Sean Hastings, an NRA member
attending the event on that day. Please take the
stand Mr. Hastings.

> *Sean Hastings walks up to the
> stand and takes a seat in the
> witness chair as the Bailiff
> approaches with the Bible.*

BAILIFF

Please place your right hand on the bible and
repeat after me, I, Sean Hastings, swear to tell
the whole truth and nothing but the truth, so
help me God.

> *Sean Hastings repeats the vow
> and takes a seat as Attorney
> Pantovere approaches the
> stand.*

MICHAEL PANTOVERE

Mr. Hastings, you were present for the NRA rally here in Arlington, VA on May 5, 2018, correct sir?

SEAN HASTINGS

Yes, I was at the rally.

MICHAEL PANTOVERE

Were you alone or did anyone else join you for the event?

SEAN HASTINGS

My brother Richard was with me.

MICHAEL PANTOVERE

I see and was your brother also an NRA member?

SEAN HASTINGS

Yes sir, he was.

MICHAEL PANTOVERE

And can you tell me what happened during your attendance at the event?

SEAN HASTINGS

Certainly. We were standing in an area that seemed under control and well behaved. There had been some conflict breaking out after the third speaker took the stage but for the most part, everyone around us seemed peaceful and respectful.

MICHAEL PANTOVERE

I see. Then what happened when Dwayne LaFollett took the stage?

SEAN HASTINGS

Well, it was calm at first but then he started to get the crowd really riled up!

MICHAEL PANTOVERE

I see. Please continue.

SEAN HASTINGS

While we were there to show our support of the NRA, we weren't there to engage in any type of inflammatory behavior or to engage in violence of any sort. Some people had already been hurt prior to this display. That's when we decided to leave.

MICHAEL PANTOVERE

I see. So, you were leaving the event and what happened next?

SEAN HASTINGS

That's when gunfire broke out from a building somewhere across the street and mass panic followed. Everyone was screaming and running. People were getting trampled on as everyone ran for cover.

MICHAEL PANTOVERE

Did either you or your brother get hurt?

SEAN HASTINGS

(getting visibly emotional and
choking up)

Yes sir, I was hit twice by bullets in my left
arm but...

(struggling to speak)

But Rick took several bullets to the chest and
he went down hard.

(openly crying)

I threw myself on top of him to try to stop him
from getting hit anymore but... It was too late.
He died on the scene.

MICHAEL PANTOVERE

I'm sorry for your loss, Mr. Hastings. Please
take a minute to collect your thoughts. Take
your time.

(pauses for effect)

Your Honor, let me share some disturbing facts
with the court. Heather Sher, a Florida
radiologist, wrote an article after her
experience in treating some of the Parkland
victims. The article explains that wounds
incurred by bullets fired from an AR-15 are
drastically different than those from bullets
fired from a handgun. Bullets from an AR-15
travel three times faster and impart more than

three times the energy, shredding organs and causing tissue damage several inches from its path. Exit wounds can be the size of an orange.

(pauses for effect)

Please continue, Mr. Hastings.

SEAN HASTINGS

Thank you. I still can't believe my big brother is dead. I looked up to him. He was so strong and also so kind. I miss him terribly!

MICHAEL PANTOVERE

And do you still believe in the Second Amendment and gun rights?

SEAN HASTINGS

Yes sir, I do. But I have always believed that there should be restrictions on gun ownership and universal background checks, and closing the gun show loophole. In my opinion, the two people at fault for this crime were the shooter, Harrison Culpepper and the NRA President, Dwayne Lafollett. I feel strongly that Dwayne LaFollett shares responsibility for making a situation that was already bad, much worse!

LEONARD SNAYDER

Objection! Your Honor, we don't convict someone as a result of an opinion! Move to strike that from the transcripts!

MICHAEL PANTOVERE

Your Honor! Mr. Hastings attended the event and witnessed the crowd getting out of hand. He not only got shot but his brother was murdered! His thoughts matter! He is simply stating the facts!

GRACE PORTER HAVERHILL

Overruled Mr. Snayder, I'll allow it.

MICHAEL PANTOVERE

Please continue, Mr. Hastings.

SEAN HASTINGS

Thank you. As I'm sure you are aware. It's been reported that Harrison Culpepper had a long history of spousal abuse and domestic violence and yet he was allowed to continue buying guns at a ridiculous rate. I think they said they found over 60 guns at his house, many of them just purchased over a short period of time.

MICHAEL PANTOVERE

You are correct, Mr. Hastings and I agree that those are disturbing factors that led to his killing spree. And yet, you chose not to file charges against Dwayne LaFollett in this case, correct?

SEAN HASTINGS

That is correct. I decided not to file charges, but I want my voice to be heard. Filing charges won't bring Rick back but maybe sensible gun

legislation will prevent another senseless
tragedy like this from occurring again.

MICHAEL PANTOVERE

I have nothing further Mr. Hastings. Thank you
for your time.

GRACE PORTER HAVERHILL

Mr. Snayder, are you prepared to cross?

> *Leonard Snayder stands and
> approaches the bench.*

LEONARD SNAYDER

Yes, your Honor, thank you. Mr. Hastings, first
let me say I am sorry for the loss of your
brother. But it has already been established
that this is a court of law that does not have
the authority or power to pass gun control
legislation. So while I am glad the taxpayer's
dollars allowed you an audience to voice your
concerns, we are here for a very serious matter,
to determine the innocence or guilt of a very
prominent businessman and leader of a very
important organization, Dwayne LaFollett. You
say, in your opinion, that Mr. LaFollett's
speech served to incense the crowd. Is that
correct?

SEAN HASTINGS

Yes sir, that is correct.

LEONARD SNAYDER

Do you think he had any prior knowledge or could have anticipated that Harrison Culpepper was perched in a window across the street with two semi-automatic rifles, getting ready to open fire upon the crowd?

SEAN HASTINGS

I don't know the answer to that question. I have no idea what Dwayne LaFollett knew or didn't know. It would seem unlikely that he would have prior information regarding a single member of the NRA.

MICHAEL PANTOVERE

Objection! Your Honor, the charges as stands are disorderly conduct and 17 counts of inciting a riot. We did NOT include the charge of conspiracy to riot, as in contrast to those charges that were successfully proven in your Charlottesville trial. We could not prove that Mr. LaFollett had, in any way premeditated the ensuing violence, with the now deceased Harrison Culpepper.

GRACE PORTER HAVERHILL

Sustained. There is no conspiracy charge here, Mr. Snayder.

LEONARD SNAYDER

Dwayne LaFollett did not know Mr. Culpepper personally, so it is not possible that his speech was the factor that drove Mr. Culpepper to engage in his shooting spree! LaFollett had no way of knowing Mr. Culpepper's whereabouts or possible intentions!

MICHAEL PANTOVERE

Objection! Your Honor, in that Harrison Culpepper was ultimately shot and killed in an exchange of gunfire with the Arlington Police, it will never be possible to know exactly what the reason was behind his decision to open fire upon the crowd!

GRACE PORTER HAVERHILL

Sustained! In light of Mr. Culpepper's demise, we will never have the ability to determine what it was that led him to this mass murder on May 5, 2018.

LEONARD SNAYDER

Your Honor, the point I was making and that the jury needs to understand is that Mr. Culpepper and my client, Dwayne LaFollett, were not personal acquaintances and that their only affiliation was via membership in the NRA. The only commonality here is that Mr. Culpepper was a member of the organization led by my client. I have nothing further.

MICHAEL PANTOVERE

Objection! Again, your Honor, my previous objection stands. There are no conspiracy charges here.

GRACE PORTER HAVERHILL

Sustained again! You may step down, Mr.
Hastings. Do you have anything further, Mr.
Pantovere?

MICHAEL PANTOVERE

Just one thing your Honor. I want to impress one
thing upon the jury, the thought that every
citizen of this country has the right to
DOMESTIC TRANQUILITY. It is as important of a
constitutional right as is the Second Amendment
and the right to bear arms. FDR once said, "The
deeper purpose of democratic government is to
assist as many of its citizens as possible... to
improve their conditions of life, to retain all
personal liberty WHICH DOES NOT ADVERSELY AFFECT
THEIR NEIGHBORS, and to pursue the happiness
which comes with SECURITY and an opportunity for
recreation and culture." No matter which side of
the gun control debate you are on, the citizens
that attended that rally on May 5, 2018 had the
right to do so, expecting that their security was
a given, and that an unhinged psychopath with a
history of violence wasn't waiting in a window
across the street, with two semi-automatic
rifles.

(pauses for effect)

As a country, our **DOMESTIC TRANQUILITY** is no
longer a constitutional right that we can be
assured of, until responsible gun control
legislation is enacted to help keep the Harrison
Culpeppers off the streets, with their arsenals
of weaponry, and until leadership of special
interest groups are held accountable for their
actions and for their words, that adversely
cause harm to others.

GRACE PORTER HAVERHILL

We will take a break for lunch and return by 1:15PM. Court is adjourned for now.

> *Grace POUNDS the gavel and gets up to return to her chambers.*

BAILIFF

All rise.

CUT TO:

II.7 INT. A PRIVATE DINING ROOM AT A LOCAL RESTAURANT - AFTERNOON

> *A waiter seats Dwayne LaFollett and his attorney, Leonard Snayder, handing them menus before he leaves the room.*

LEONARD SNAYDER

Hey Jason, we are on a tight schedule this afternoon and have less than an hour for lunch. Bring us both whatever your special is today, it's always outstanding!

JASON/WAITSTAFF

It's beef tips and asparagus over mushroom risotto with a burgundy reduction and a side salad.

LEONARD SNAYDER

Great! Two of those as quickly as possible with a bottle of Perrier and lemon slices.

DWAYNE LAFOLLETT

Throw in two fingers of Wild Turkey, neat, please.

JASON/WAITSTAFF

Yes sir, I'll be right back with that.

LEONARD SNAYDER

Do you really think that's a good idea today, Dwayne?

DWAYNE LAFOLLETT

It's the only thing that's going to stop me from killing your wimpy little Boy Scout ass!

Raising his voice.

What the hell do you think you are doing in there? Or should I say, NOT doing in there? My God your crosses are pathetic. He's walking all over you. Most importantly, he's walking all over me and it's MY ass that is on the line here. For a grand an hour you better step up your game, Snayder!

LEONARD SNAYDER

Calm down Dwayne and lower your voice! I've said what I needed to say and sometimes less is more in the minds of jurors.

DWAYNE LAFOLLETT

How in the hell am I supposed to trust you to
have my best interests in mind?

LEONARD SNAYDER

I've been doing this for a long time Dwayne. I
know what I'm doing. I needed to get the Police
Chief off of the stand. The jurors didn't need
to here anymore about the deaths that occurred
that day or any more about your speech.

> *Jason brings in their
> drinks/lunches and they start
> to quickly eat.*

DWAYNE LAFOLLETT

(downing his whiskey in one gulp)

You better know what you are doing cause if you
don't, you'll never work in this town again. I
promise you that. I've been doing THIS for a
long time.

CUT TO:

II.8 INT - THE RED ROOM - AFTERNOON

> *Our founding fathers are
> seated or standing at various
> points in the room.*

JOHN ADAMS

So much for your idea of a "living
Constitution," Thomas. It appears that the
passage of time has resulted in our words being

interpreted in such a manner that **DOMESTIC TRANQUILITY** is now imperiled.

THOMAS JEFFERSON

(scratching his forehead and
appearing to be lost in thought)

It seems to be that way and perilously so.

(pauses for effect)

My original proposal was that we should provide a stipulation in our Constitution for its revision at stated periods. Each generation should have the solemn opportunity to update the Constitution every nineteen or twenty years, thus allowing it to be handed on with periodical repairs from generation to generation, to the end of time.

(pauses for effect)

However, that was not the remedy that was actually incorporated into the Constitution. As it currently stands, our Constitution can only be amended by votes of 2/3 of the House and the Senate and 3/4 of state legislatures, with an end requiring consensus of such a large populace to render it all but impossible. Thankfully many states did see the benefits of allowing for periodic revisions as incorporated into their state constitutions.

JOHN ADAMS

I recall my cousin, Samuel saying, "That the said Constitution shall never be construed to prevent the people of the United States who are

PEACEABLE citizens from keeping their own arms."
Therein lies the whole paradox - some measure of
control must be taken to keep armaments out of
the hands of hoodlums and despots.

ALEXANDER HAMILTON

Little more can reasonably be aimed at, with
respect to the people at large, than to have
them properly armed and equipped.

AARON BURR

Posterity will make you regret your viewpoint
someday.

      (said half under his breath and
        chuckling to himself)

THOMAS JEFFERSON

On every occasion...let us carry ourselves back
to the time when the Constitution was adopted,
recollect the spirit manifested in the debates,
and instead of trying to force what meaning may
be squeezed out of the text, or invented against
it,instead let us conform to the probable one in
which it was passed.

        (pauses for effect)

These modern-day legislators cannot hide behind
the dead hand of the past as an excuse to not
introduce and pass intelligent laws to safeguard
the lives of their constituents. Why, without
safety there can be no **LIBERTY!**

JAMES MADISON

The scenarios, as explained in this current court case are more disturbing than any set of events we could have ever anticipated in the drafting of our founding principles! **It all defies common sense! Why, it defies our founding principles!**

(pauses for effect)

It is the job of, why the sworn responsibility of Congress to uphold and defend our Constitution! As elected officials, their duty is to represent the interests of their respective constituents, not to line their coffers with gold from special interest groups that help them to get re-elected!

GEORGE WASHINGTON

You are quite right, James! It sounds like the majority of the populace are in favor of legislation to enforce stricter and more sensible regulations regarding gun purchases and ownership!

(pauses for effect)

How is it that Congress is functioning as the bottleneck, versus the mechanism for change, as demanded by their constituents? It has clearly become a partisan issue and that was always a penultimate concern of mine, the potentially devastating ramifications of rivalry and discontent amongst parties!

ALEXANDER HAMILTON

In a country where freedom of choice was the basis for our foundation, a sensible man simply acts in response to his own conscience, whatever that is defined to be. To participate, or not to participate? These are the options of a truly free-thinking and emancipated mindset!

AARON BURR

For the love of God, Alexander, our brothers are quite eloquent and speak well of the need for this current generation to examine these instances of mass casualties and adapt the written word, the law to the thing. It was not possible to anticipate the rapid advancements in weaponry that would then result in unintended and grossly exaggerated protections attached to our founding principles, in an effort to explain away such carnage.

ALEXANDER HAMILTON

(said with contempt and glancing fervently at Burr)

Good gentlemen, do not let yourself be fooled by the cooperative appearance of such a snake in the grass, as there can be no kernel in this light nut; the soul of this man is his clothes.

AARON BURR

(Spoken with mutual contempt)

Why yes, Alexander, I see a good amendment of life in thee, from praying to purse-taking.

ALEXANDER HAMILTON

I would be wise of my senses and short of thy
tongue, Master Burr, as my opinion and
reputation within the high offices and law-
making committees of these colonies is quite
renowned and high, indeed. Your insufferable ego
and feckless intentions will render you
unsuitable and without the necessary backing for
the offices that you so falsely aspire to. Thou
art unfit for any place but hell.

AARON BURR

You may well use your substantial influence and
clout to block my political ambitions, Hamilton,
and impede my further successes, but in
retrospect I say just one thing, you ireful
bastard.

ALEXANDER HAMILTON

And pray tell, what might that be, Master Burr?

AARON BURR

Dueling is not your forte....

> *The stage darkens and the*
> *curtain falls for a brief*
> *moment.*

CUT TO:

II.9 INT. - COURTROOM - AFTERNOON

> *Throngs of protesters remain*
> *gathered outside the courtroom*
> *representing both sides of the*
> *argument, gun rights and gun*

control advocates. There is
mass confusion and shouting,
with each side holding banners
espousing their views.

BAILIFF

All rise. The Honorable Grace Porter Haverhill
is now presiding.

Grace enters the courtroom
from her chambers, takes her
seat, and POUNDS the gavel.

GRACE PORTER HAVERHILL

We will continue to hear ongoing arguments in
The United States District Court of The Eastern
District of The Commonwealth of Virginia v.
Dwayne LaFollett as a result of the May 5, 2018
NRA rally here in Arlington. Mr. Snayder, your
witness.

LEONARD SNAYDER

Thank you, your Honor. I would like to call
Sarah Pinckney, a gun control advocate and May
5th, 2018 rally attendee to the stand.

GRACE PORTER HAVERHILL

Proceed, please.

Sarah Pinckney walks up to the
stand and takes a seat in the
witness chair as the Bailiff
approaches with the Bible.

BAILIFF

Please place your right hand on the bible and repeat after me, I, Sarah Pinckney, swear to tell the whole truth and nothing but the truth, so help me God.

Sarah Pinckney repeats the vow and takes a seat as Attorney Leonard Snayder approaches the bench.

LEONARD SNAYDER

Good afternoon, Mrs. Pinckney. Thank you for testifying this afternoon.

SARAH PINCKNEY

You're welcome, Attorney Snayder. I am happy to share my experience.

LEONARD SNAYDER

So, to confirm, you attended the May 5th, 2018 NRA rally in Arlington, VA correct?

SARAH PINCKNEY

Yes sir, I was there.

LEONARD SNAYDER

And what side of this debate are you on Mam and what was the decision that made you decide to attend this rally?

SARAH PINCKNEY

I am a gun control advocate and have routinely participated in gun control rallies for years, in DC, VA, MD and across the country.

LEONARD SNAYDER

Ok, so you were there not to endorse the NRA but to oppose the NRA and its stance on gun rights?

SARAH PINCKNEY

Correct. I live in the inner city of Baltimore. My family and friends have seen gang violence and just plain old random gun violence take too many of our family and friends away from us. We have seen too many deaths as a result of senseless gun violence.

LEONARD SNAYDER

Thank you. As the rally continued and prior to Dwayne LaFolett taking the stage what did you witness and what were your concerns?

SARAH PINCKNEY

Well, we was on the other side of the barricades and the police seemed to be doing a pretty good job of keeping the peace between the two sides until that third nasty speaker came along.

LEONARD SNAYDER

The "whiny little bitches" speaker?

SARAH PINCKNEY

Yeah, that's right. So, I'se listening to him rant on and I don't agree with what he's saying at all and neither do my homeys, my sisters, who were with me at the rally.

LEONARD SNAYDER

So, what did you do next, Mam?

SARAH PINCKNEY

Well, I walked over to the front of the barricade and I respectfully asked one of them NRA members for a word.

LEONARD SNAYDER

So, you just ventured to ask the closest NRA member for a word? No fear of retaliation? No fear of an altercation?

SARAH PINCKNEY

That's right. I'm surrounded by the Po Po and in my man Dr. King's spirit, if I can't reach out and ask for some peaceful conversation, then I am missing an opportunity.

LEONARD SNAYDER

Ok, so you reached out an olive branch to an NRA member in hopes of having a meaningful conversation. What happened next?

SARAH PINCKNEY

Well, much to my surprise, that's exactly what happened. It was a tense conversation to begin with for sure, but after 5 or 10 minutes of explaining our sides to each other, we seemed to come to a middle ground. Not an agreement, but a place where we could both understand each other's point of view.

LEONARD SNAYDER

How did that feel to you Mam?

SARAH PINCKNEY

Well, it was a little bit of a breakthrough. Seeing that all it might take is a bit of listening to each other instead of yelling at each other.

LEONARD SNAYDER

Very good. I venture that you did not have a gun on your person?

SARAH PINCKNEY

No, you are correct. I do not own any guns. But during Dwayne LaFollett's speech, this woman got real fired up and I just kind of stood there and watched her.

LEONARD SNAYDER

I see. What happened next Mam?

SARAH PINCKNEY

That's when the shots started firing down from the rooftop across the street and everyone was in a panic. This lady, I didn't even know her name, got hit. We was all down on the ground by then hoping to somehow take cover but it was a blood bath. She was bleeding out and me and my friends tried to make tourniquets out of pieces of our clothes to save her, but there would be no saving her. I've never been quite that close to seeing someone when they're dying. I hope I never have to see that again.

LEONARD SNAYDER

That must have been awful. I am sorry that you had to witness that carnage. Mam, who do you think is responsible for the events of that awful afternoon? Can you look at my client, Dwayne LaFollett, as the President of the National Rifle Association and pin the blame on him? Can you?

SARAH PINCKNEY

No sir, I cannot! He was just doing what the master of the ceremony is supposed to be doing when they gets people riled up and invested in supportin their cause! And I was there to oppose them. He was annoyin and I wish I could have shut him up. I wish I could blame it on him, but I just can't cause it don't seem right! Ain't nobody with a crystal ball to know there is some crazy man with assault rifles in the top floor of a hotel across the street. I came there to stand in peace and to try to find a common ground. I actually think we done that prior to this kind lady being killed in cold blood. Makes

me think that so much more could be accomplished
if we approached our opposition with peace in
our hearts instead of guns in our hands. Uh huh,
Dr. King tried to teach us all a thing or two
and it has been lost on this current generation.

LEONARD SNAYDER

Thank you, Mam. I have nothing further.

GRACE PORTER HAVERHILL

Thank you, Mr. Snayder. Mr. Pantovere are you
ready to cross?

MICHAEL PANTOVERE

Yes, your Honor, thank you!

> *Attorney Pantovere rises from
> his seat and approaches the
> bench*

GRACE PORTER HAVERHILL

Proceed!

MICHAEL PANTOVERE

Mrs. Pinckney, thank you for your appearance in
this court today. I cannot imagine the trauma
you witnessed at this rally on May 5, 2018. You
stated that you did not see the course of events
that unfolded as being a responsibility of
Dwayne LaFollett, correct?

SARAH PINCKNEY

Yes, I said that.

MICHAEL PANTOVERE

And yet, in all of your years of attending
rallies and events, have you ever witnessed
being part of a crowd that was being so
willfully encouraged to take a very open stance
against gun control advocacy and gun control
legislation, in general?

SARAH PINCKNEY

Well, if you put it like that, no. I always
think that both sides have their rights to
believe. But, I will say that this rally, the
speakers at this rally, definitely seemed to
want to pit the two sides against each other and
that made me uncomfortable. You don't want to
create such a tense situation at a rally where
the majority of people have guns.

MICHAEL PANTOVERE

Especially when you consider that there had
already been a number of altercations serious
enough for some rally participants to require
medical attention, being taken to area emergency
rooms via ambulance, by the time Dwayne
LaFollett took to the stage to speak!

SARAH PINCKNEY

That's true too! I guess when you lay it out
like that, the speaker's words were seeming to
fan the flames a bit!

MICHAEL PANTOVERE

You might even say that Dwayne LaFollett's speech was downright reckless!

LEONARD SNAYDER

Objection! Your Honor, he is trying to put words in the witness's mouth!

GRACE PORTER HAVERHILL

Sustained! Come on Mr. Pantovere, you know better than that!

MICHAEL PANTOVERE

I'm sorry your Honor, I'll rephrase. Mrs. Pinckney, in your opinion, do you think that Dwayne LaFollett needed to repeatedly be shouting, "GUNS, GUNS, GUNS, we need more GUNS," in the interests of keeping the peace at this rally?

SARAH PINCKNEY

Well no, I guess it was a little bit foolish. I guess he just wasn't thinkin in the heat of the moment and all.

MICHAEL PANTOVERE

Thank you, Mrs. Pinckney. I have nothing further.

GRACE PORTER HAVERHILL

Thank you, Mrs. Pinckney, you may step down. Mr. Snayder, do you have anything that you would like to add counselor before this witness steps down?

LEONARD SNAYDER

Yes, your Honor.

GRACE PORTER HAVERHILL

Proceed!

LEONARD SNAYDER

Ladies and gentlemen of the jury, after listening to this witnesses closing comments, I would like to quote the late great philosopher, Voltaire, who so eloquently said, "I wholly disapprove of what you say, and will defend to the death your right to say it."

(pauses for effect)

I have nothing further until we get started again in the morning, your Honor.

GRACE PORTER HAVERHILL

Thank you, Mr. Snayder. The witness may step down. Court is adjourned until tomorrow morning at 9:00AM.

                    Grace POUNDS the gavel and
                    gathers her papers to step
                    down from her bench.

CUT TO:

II.10 INT. - "THE RED ROOM" - SAME TIME

> *James Madison, Thomas*
> *Jefferson, George Washington,*
> *Alexander Hamilton, and John*
> *Adams are seated or standing*
> *at various places in the room.*

JAMES MADISON

Our First Amendment freedoms give us the right
to think what we like and say what we please.
And if we the people are to govern ourselves, we
must have these rights, even if they are misused
by a minority.

THOMAS JEFFERSON

Yes, James I agree with you wholeheartedly. In
my first inaugural address I stated, we are all
Republicans, we are all Federalists. If there be
any among us who would wish to dissolve this
Union or to change its Republican form, let them
stand undisturbed as monuments of the safety
with which error of opinion may be tolerated
where reason is left free to combat it.

(pauses for effect)

But let me also say again... That laws and
institutions must go hand in hand with the
progress of the human mind. Some men look at
Constitutions with sanctimonious reverence...
too sacred to be touched.

(pauses for effect)

But we made the assumption that future
generations would call upon their legislators
and state governments to pass laws of common
sense. In an effort to acknowledge and take into
consideration advancements and modernizations
that must be regulated and kept in check, so as
not to threaten **DOMESTIC TRANQUILITY,** which is a
critical piece of the Preamble of our
Constitution.

JAMES MADISON

Yes, Thomas, I agree with you! In looking back
at our framing years, we created departments to
help establish and maintain **JUSTICE** and to
defend our Country and provide for general
welfare, but it seems that we did not create an
adequate regulatory body to help ensure **DOMESTIC
TRANQUILITY**.

(pauses for effect)

Why, I listen to this case at hand and hear of
the horrors of these human massacres that have
become a daily occurrence in this country of our
making, these United States of America. It seems
quite evident that we were remiss in taking into
consideration the advancements in weaponry and
at its most basic, the deterioration of the
human psyche, that could have the most grave
consequences for future generations. The
propensity of our citizenry to commit such
heinous crimes was unforeseeable.

GEORGE WASHINGTON

Why James, be not too hard on yourself! **Man, how
could we have ever anticipated advances in
weaponry that would provide for a single weapon**

or two to be equivalent to the attack of a full-on infantry assault?

(pauses for effect)

We relied on pistols, muskets, and canons. How could we ever contemplate such advances and the increased force of weaponry?

(said as an aside and with a degree of humor)

I mean, we were certainly prescient and sometimes quite prophetic in framing our Constitution and in anticipating critical factors to help safeguard our democracy for future generations, but we just couldn't foresee it all! The propensity for violence amongst our citizenry could by no means have been anticipated in the written word of our founding principles and documents.

THOMAS JEFFERSON

It behooves every man who values **LIBERTY** of conscience for himself, to resist invasions of it in the case of others: or their case may, by change of circumstances, become his own.

ALEXANDER HAMILTON

It is a truth, which the experience of ages has attested, that the people are always most in danger when the means of injuring their rights are in the possession of those whom they entertain the least suspicion.

JOHN ADAMS

Why, our families, our communities, our schools
and places of worship and public gathering
grounds should not be in constant fear of
assault and blood shed! There can be no **DOMESTIC
TRANQUILITY** in a people that live in constant
FEAR.

(pauses for effect)

LIBERTY must at all hazards be supported. We
have a right to it, derived from our Maker. But
if we had not, our Fathers have earned and
bought it for us, at the expense of their ease,
their estates, their pleasure, and their blood.

JAMES MADISON

In Europe, charters of **LIBERTY** have been granted
by power. America has set the example... of
charters of power granted by **LIBERTY**. This
revolution in the practice of the world, may,
with an honest praise, be pronounced the most
triumphant epoch of its history, and the most
consoling presage of happiness. But there can be
no true and lasting happiness without **DOMESTIC
TRANQUILITY**. The sense of peace that comes with
knowing that you, your family, and your
citizenry live in safety.

(pauses for effect)

The powers delegated by the Constitution to the
federal government are few and defined. Those
which are to remain in the state governments are
numerous and indefinite.

CUT TO:

II.11 INT. - COURTROOM - AFTERNOON

> *Throngs of protesters remain*
> *gathered outside the courtroom*
> *representing both sides of the*
> *argument, gun rights and gun*
> *control advocates. There is*
> *mass confusion and shouting,*
> *with each side holding banners*
> *espousing their views.*

BAILIFF

All rise. The Honorable Grace Porter Haverhill
is now presiding.

> *Grace enters the courtroom*
> *from her chambers, takes her*
> *seat, and POUNDS the gavel.*

GRACE PORTER HAVERHILL

We will continue to hear ongoing arguments in
The Eastern District Court of The Commonwealth
of Virginia v. Dwayne LaFollett, as a result of
the May 5, 2018 NRA rally here in Arlington, VA.
Mr. Snayder, are you ready to resume on behalf
of the defense?

> *Snayder stands.*

LEONARD SNAYDER

Yes, thank you, your Honor. Ladies and gentlemen
of the jury, my client Dwayne LaFollett was in
no way inciting a riot and as head of the NRA,
was only doing what every good leader does and
that is, to educate and disseminate information

to his members, to encourage camaraderie and continue to grow the membership base.

(pauses for effect)

I say it again, he was doing nothing more than exercising his First Amendment right of free speech and his Second Amendment right to bear arms.

(pauses for effect)

I would like to call a witness to the stand, your Honor.

GRACE PORTER HAVERHILL

Proceed counselor.

LEONARD SNAYDER

The defense calls Robert Ring to the stand.

> *Robert Ring walks up to the stand and takes a seat in the witness chair as the Bailiff approaches with the Bible.*

BAILIFF

Please place your right hand on the bible and repeat after me, I, Robert Ring, swear to tell the whole truth and nothing but the truth, so help me God.

> *Robert Ring repeats the vow and takes a seat as Attorney Leonard Snayder approaches the bench.*

ROBERT RING

I do!

GRACE PORTER HAVERHILL

You may be seated, Mr. Ring.

LEONARD SNAYDER

Mr. Ring, were you the speaker that spoke immediately before the defendant, Dwayne Lafollett, at the Arlington rally?

ROBERT RING

Yes sir, I was.

LEONARD SNAYDER

And what was your informed and firsthand assessment of the demeanor and mood of the crowd during your speech?

ROBERT RING

The gun rights advocates certainly outnumbered the gun control advocates but it was not a scene that was out of the ordinary for some of our rallies. There will always be protesters, always dissenters, but that is their right as well.

LEONARD SNAYDER

And in your speech, you did refer to the Parkland school shooting survivors as, "whiny little bitches looking for their fifteen minutes of fame," correct?

ROBERT RING

Yes, that is correct. I was doing nothing more than exercising my First Amendment right to voice my opinion. Based on the applause that I was getting; it was clear that the crowd was on my side and shared in my opinion.

LEONARD SNAYDER

Some unrest developed during your speech and medics were called to the scene, is that right, Mr. Ring?

ROBERT RING

Yes, that is correct. But during my years as a member of the leadership team at the NRA, it is not the first time that I have experienced conflict or differences of opinions. That is exactly what our First Amendment protects.

LEONARD SNAYDER

So, the fact that some skirmishes broke out that required medical attention was neither a red flag or siren for dialing back the content of the remains of your speech, or an imminent concern for my client as he took to the stage?

ROBERT RING

No sir, not in my opinion. There will always be differences in opinions when you gather 1,000 people to celebrate the sanctity of gun rights and gun ownership.

LEONARD SNAYDER

Thank you, Mr. Ring. I have nothing further.

GRACE PORTER HAVERHILL

Mr. Pantovere, are you ready to cross?

> *Michael Pantovere stands and approaches the witness.*

MICHAEL PANTOVERE

Ladies and gentlemen of the jury, I need to remind opposing counsel of the findings of Brandenburg v. Ohio once more. The Supreme Court held that speech that is directed to inciting or producing imminent lawless action and is likely to incite or produce such action is NOT protected by the First Amendment.

(pauses for effect)

For all intents and purposes, the defendant might as well have been yelling, "fire," in a crowded theater.

LEONARD SNAYDER

Objection, your Honor! Counsel has no way of knowing what my client's intent was and he is referencing an entirely different scenario!

GRACE PORTER HAVERHILL

Sustained! Mr. Pantovere, would you like to rephrase?

MICHAEL PANTOVERE

Yes, thank you, your Honor. Quite simply, the
mood of the crowd was growing increasingly
agitated and aggressive and there is no logical
reason why the defendant would then proceed to
take the stage and continue to fan the flames.
There were already ambulances and medics on the
scene and injuries had been sustained.

(pauses for effect)

If that isn't inflammatory speech leading to
imminent lawless action, then I don't know what
is.

GRACE PORTER HAVERHILL

Thank you, Mr. Pantovere. The witness may step
down. Do you have anything further, counselor?

MICHAEL PANTOVERE

Yes, your Honor. Let me make a comparison. The
right to drive a car isn't included in our
Constitution or the Bill of Rights. But since
the invention of automobiles, common sense laws
and safeguards were enacted to help ensure that
every person in this country must pass a driving
test to verify the most basic of driving
abilities are intact and that our citizen's
automobiles are licensed, registered, insured
and inspected and these safeguards must be
renewed and updated periodically. Why not guns?

(pauses for effect)

As of 2015, more Americans are killed by a gun
than are killed in car crashes! In 1995, it only
took one kook to try to blow up a plane with a

shoe bomb. Now we all have to take off our shoes
as a precautionary screening measure before
boarding a plane!

(pauses for effect)

You have to get a license to be able to hunt and
yet such restrictions aren't required to
regulate the gun that you use? It is basic logic
that our states take every measure to ensure
that our citizens are competent prior to them
getting behind the wheel of a two-ton
automobile. There certainly have been some
tragic accidents involving several automobiles.
When the tragedy results in multiple human
fatalities, it is typically limited to one or
some or all of the individuals driving or
occupying the vehicles or being in the vicinity
of the collision. The recent mass shooting at
the outdoor music festival in Las Vegas resulted
in 58 deaths and 413 wounded in a less than 5
minute shooting spree, with two AR-15 rifles,
modified with bump stocks. Common sense gun
legislation needs to be enacted to protect the
innocent. Only then can **DOMESTIC TRANQUILITY** be
restored and that IS a most basic right given to
every citizen of these United States by our
Constitution.

(pauses for effect)

We have a minority of our population that are so
consumed with protecting an amendment that was
never intended to be anything more than a
restrictive clause on the rights of the federal
government and that in no way "granted" any
types of rights to our citizenry. They now stand
in the way of allowing our governments to
provide communities the necessary legislation to
help ensure that our communities, our schools,

our houses of worship and our public gathering
spaces are as safe as possible from the threat
of gun violence. When this much needed
legislation is finally allowed to be enacted,
our communities will once more become the safe
havens intended for us by our founding fathers,
where **DOMESTIC TRANQUILITY** will once more
prevail.

(pauses for effect)

This country was founded on the basic, core
principles in our Constitution of **LIFE**, **LIBERTY**
and the pursuit of **HAPPINESS**. So, it stands to
reason that protecting the lives of our
citizenry is a basic core function of our state
and federal governments. These contemporary,
persistent arguments for gun rights and the
exaggerated interpretations of what the Second
Amendment protects are incompatible with our
Constitution and the actual intention of The
Bill of Rights. They are incompatible with
LIBERTY and annihilate our ability to safeguard
our democracy.

(pauses for effect)

Common sense legislation regarding gun control
initiatives have been stalled in the Senate now
for years. How many mass shootings has our
country had to endure during those wasted
months of partisan stranglehold? How many more
people need to get senselessly and tragically
massacred before we take some action? This
should not be an issue decided along party
lines. The sanctity of human life should be
equally important to every elected official
whether he or she be a Republican or a
Democrat. The only meaningful gun control

legislation that has been passed recently is the ban on the sale of bump stocks.

LEONARD SNAYDER

Objection, your Honor! Counsel is grandstanding and positing his opinions and those of his clients. We aren't hear for a refresher course on the Constitution or the Bill of Rights cloaked behind a veil of patriotism

GRACE PORTER HAVERHILL

Sustained! Mr. Pantovere, where are you going with this?

MICHAEL PANTOVERE

Your Honor, counsel for the defense and his client and his witnesses keep on trying to claim that they are just exercising their First and Second Amendment rights and that their rights are being threatened or invalidated.

(pauses for effect)

What I'm saying, IS, that if we really want to correctly interpret the wording of the First and Second Amendments, nowhere in the verbiage of these amendments, does it "GRANT" anybody anything! What these two amendments, as well as all of the rest of the amendments do, is restrain the power of the federal government regarding the enumerated rights. The right to free speech and the right to bear arms are rights granted independently of the Constitution and The Bill of Rights. Typically, these rights live in most state constitutions and above and beyond that, they are inherently the rights given to mankind.

(pauses for effect)

The purpose of our Bill of Rights was to incorporate into our Constitution, a set of rights that the federal government cannot infringe upon. Every amendment in the Bill of Rights is either declaratory or restrictive but **NONE** of them grant anybody the **RIGHT** to anything. The right to freedom of speech, freedom of the press, freedom of religion and the right to bear arms are God given rights we are born with, but they are not absolutes and are restricted by the powers given to state governments.

LEONARD SNAYDER

Objection your Honor! Is opposing counsel quite through espousing his interpretation of our founding documents? Who needs law school or Congress or The Supreme Court? Why, we have our very own "Justice" Pantovere to school us on all of the finite points of the meanings behind our democracy, our Constitution, and the Bill of Rights. Why, I'm just waiting for him to start singing "The Star-Spangled Banner."

(there is laughter in the
courtroom)

GRACE PORTER HAVERHILL

You're a funny guy, Mr. Snayder. Do you have anything further to share, Mr. Pantovere?

MICHAEL PANTOVERE

Since we're in such a joking mood here this afternoon, Will Rogers once said, "Congress is going to start tinkering with the Ten Commandments just as soon as they can find someone in Washington who has read them."

GRACE PORTER HAVERHILL

Touché, Mr. Pantovere. Thank you, counselors. Court is adjourned for the day. We will get started again tomorrow morning at 9:15AM.

> *Grace POUNDS the gavel and gathers her paperwork. She steps down from the bench to return to her chambers.*

BAILIFF

All rise.

CUT TO:

III.12 INT. - "THE RED ROOM" - SAME TIME

> *James Madison, Thomas Jefferson, George Washington, and John Adams are seated or standing at various places in the room.*

THOMAS JEFFERSON

I know of no safe depository of the ultimate powers of society but the people themselves; and if we think them not enlightened enough to exercise their control with a wholesome discretion, the remedy is not to take it from

them, but to inform their discretion by
education.

(pauses for effect)

A wise and frugal government, which shall
RESTRAIN MEN FROM INJURING ONE ANOTHER, shall
leave them otherwise free to regulate their own
pursuits of industry and improvement, and shall
not take from the mouth of labor the bread it
has earned. This is the sum of good government.

JOHN ADAMS

Fear is the foundation of most governments.

THOMAS JEFFERSON

Sometimes it is said that man cannot be trusted
with the government of himself. Can he, then, be
trusted with the government of others?

GEORGE WASHINGTON

The aggregate happiness of the society which is
best promoted by the practice of a virtuous
policy, is or ought to be, the end of all
government.

THOMAS JEFFERSON

But I also clearly stated that it is time
enough, for the rightful purposes of civil
government, for its officers **TO INTERFERE** when
principles break out into overt acts against
PEACE and **GOOD ORDER.**

(pauses for effect)

Why it certainly sounds like this Republican
faction has chosen to not act in the best
interests of their constituents by failing to
pass critical legislation to help prevent and
mitigate these violent massacres.

                    JAMES MADISON

One would posit how these elected officials
remain in their seats with such abandonment of
their sworn duties.

                (pauses for effect)

A remedy must be obtained from the people, who
can by the election of more faithful
representatives, annul the acts of the usurpers.

                    JOHN ADAMS

If the people never, jointly nor severally,
think of usurping the rights of others, what
occasion can there be for any government at all?

                (pauses for effect)

Is not every crime a usurpation over other men's
rights? There are some few, indeed, whose whole
lives and conversations show that, in every
thought, word and action, they conscientiously
respect the rights of others.

                (pauses for effect)

There is a larger body still, who, in the
general tenor of their thoughts and actions,
discover similar principles and feelings, yet
frequently err. A vast majority frequently
transgress; and almost all, confine their

benevolence to their families, relations,
personal friends, parish, village, city, county,
province, and that very few, indeed, extend it
impartially to the whole community.

(pauses for effect)

Accordingly, it would seem that some provision
should be made in the Constitution, in favor of
JUSTICE, to compel all to respect the common
right, the public good, the universal law, in
preference to all private and partial
considerations.

ALEXANDER HAMILTON

Political factions can be one of the most fatal
diseases of popular government.

JOHN ADAMS

Can you find a people who will never be divided
in opinion? Who will be always unanimous? The
people of Rome were divided as all people ever
have been and will be, into a variety of parties
and factions.

(pauses for effect)

A popular party are apt to think that the rules
of veracity and candor may be dispensed with,
and that deceit and violence may without any
scruple, be employed in their own favor.

(pauses for effect)

With less honor and dignity to maintain than
their adversaries, they are less afraid of
imputations that detract from either; and their

leaders, supported by the voice of the more
numerous party, are less apprehensive of evil
fame.

JAMES MADISON

Complaints are everywhere heard from our most
considerate and virtuous citizens... That our
governments are too unstable; that the public
good is disregarded in the conflicts of rival
parties; and that measures are too often
decided, not according to the rules of justice,
and the rights of the minor party; but by the
superior force of an interested and over-
bearing majority.

(pauses for effect)

However anxiously we may wish that these
complaints had no foundation, the evidence of
known facts will not permit us to deny that they
are in some degree true.

THOMAS JEFFERSON

Men by their constitutions are naturally divided
into two parties.

GEORGE WASHINGTON

The common and continual mischiefs of the spirit
of party are sufficient to make it the interest
and duty of a wise people to discourage it and
restrain it. Let me...warn you in the most
solemn manner against the baneful effects of the
spirit of party generally.

(pauses for effect)

The spirit, unfortunately, is inseparable from our nature, having its root in the strongest passions of the human minds, so I quite agree with you on that, Thomas. It exists under different shapes in all governments, more or less stifles, controlled, or repressed; but, in those of the popular form, it is seen in its greatest rankness, and is truly their worst enemy.

(pauses for effect)

The alternate domination of one faction over another, sharpened by the spirit of revenge, natural to party dissension, which in different ages and countries has perpetrated the most horrid enormities, is itself a frightful despotism. The disorders and miseries, which result, gradually incline the minds of men to seek security and repose in the absolute power of an individual; and sooner or later the chief of some prevailing faction, more able or more fortunate than his competitors, turns the disposition to the purposes of his own elevation, on the ruins of Public **LIBERTY**.

THOMAS JEFFERSON

I never submitted the whole system of my opinions to the creed of any party of men whatever...if I could not go to Heaven but with a party, I would not go there at all.

GEORGE WASHINGTON

It serves always to distract the Public Councils and enfeeble the Public Administration. It agitates the Community with ill-founded jealousies and false alarms; kindles the

animosity of one part against another, foments
occasionally riot and insurrection. It opens the
door to foreign influence and corruption, which
finds a facilitated access to the government
itself through the channels of party passions.
Thus the policy and the will of one country are
subjected to the policy and will of another.

JAMES MADISON

LIBERTY is to faction, what air is to fire, an
aliment without which it instantly expires.

GEORGE WASHINGTON

The basis of our political systems is the right
of the people to make and alter their
constitutions of government. But the
Constitution which at any time exists, until
changed by an explicit and authentic act of the
whole people, is sacredly obligatory upon all.

(pauses for effect)

The Constitution is the guide which I will never
abandon.

CUT TO:

II.13 INT. - COURTROOM - MORNING

*There are throngs of
protesters gathered outside
the courtroom representing
both sides of the argument,
gun rights and gun control
advocates. There is mass
confusion and shouting, with*

112

> *each side holding banners*
> *espousing their views.*

BAILIFF

All rise. The Honorable Grace Porter Haverhill
is now presiding.

> *Grace enters the courtroom*
> *from her chambers, takes her*
> *seat, and POUNDS the gavel.*

GRACE PORTER HAVERHILL

Be seated please. Today we are gathered to hear
closing arguments in The Eastern District Court
of The Commonwealth of Virginia v. Dwayne
LaFollett. Mr. Pantovere, Mr. Snayder, are you
ready to get started?

> *Both attorneys stand and speak*
> *in unison.*

MICHAEL PANTOVERE/LEONARD
SNAYDER

We are, your Honor!

GRACE PORTER HAVERHILL

Very well, Mr. Pantovere, please proceed with
closing arguments.

MICHAEL PANTOVERE

Thank you, your Honor. Ladies and gentlemen of
the jury, we are here today to try to get some
JUSTICE, some redemption, if possible, for Mr.

Owens and his family and all of the other victims of this senseless mass shooting here in our city. They've become so commonplace and we need to try to figure out reasonable safeguards to ensure that we are as safe as possible within our communities. I'm a father of two. It is a helpless feeling when one of the first items on your back to school shopping list for your kids are bullet proof backpacks! Our children are now taught first aid procedures on helping to prevent their classmates from bleeding out in the event of a school shooting.

> *He puts his head in his hands*
> *for a moment and looks around*
> *the courtroom*

Where is our **LIBERTY**? Where is our **DOMESTIC TRANQUILITY**? What happened to **LIFE, LIBERTY,** and the **PURSUIT OF HAPPINESS**? No, it's more important for our senators to placate special interest groups than to heed the concerns of their constituents back home who are burying their children, their brothers and sisters, mothers, and fathers. Mr. LaFollett and the NRA need to take heed.

(pauses for effect)

In the 1951 ruling of Feiner v. New York, Feiner was giving a speech to about 80 people in Syracuse, NY, encouraging black people to take up weapons and fight for their rights against white people. The police were called, and the racially mixed crowd asked for the police to ask Feiner to end his speech, which he refused to do, after being asked to do so by the police three times. There were threats of violence and unrest in the crowd. Mr. Feiner was politely asked to refrain from further speaking twice more before arrested, given a fair trial, and convicted accordingly. The primary holding here was that the First Amendment permits the government to take action against speech when there is clear and present danger that it will cause a disturbance of the peace.

(pauses for effect)

In another similar ruling, Cantwell v. Connecticut stated, "the offense known as breach of the peace embraces a great variety of conduct destroying or menacing public order and tranquility. It includes not only violent acts but acts and words likely to produce violence in others." Mr. Lafollett's inflammatory speech, actions and suggestions were far more egregious than the previous precedent set in Feiner or Cantwell.

LEONARD SNAYDER

Objection! Your Honor, I don't see how these cases can be used as precedence, when Chief Miller testified that he did not give any type of verbal warning to the defendant. Not once, twice, or three times, so I don't see how this can be applicable?

GRACE PORTER HAVERHILL

Mr. Pantovere? Your response?

MICHAEL PANTOVERE

Your Honor, the case at hand had already surpassed the urgency of the Feiner case, in that injuries had been sustained and medical attention was required. Are we going to now try to assess blame to the police department? Any person of normal intelligence should have had the capacity to assess the situation and speak accordingly.

GRACE PORTER HAVERHILL

Overruled! I'll allow it. Please continue Mr. Pantovere.

MICHAEL PANTOVERE

Let us now shift our focus to the charges of inciting a riot and violating the federal riots act and the intent to promote and encourage a riot.

(pauses for effect)

Back in 1969, the evening after the assassination of Dr. Martin Luther King Jr., rioting and subsequent looting broke out in D.C., as it did in many other cities across the U.S. Charles Matthews was initially convicted of three crimes, but only charged with petit larceny and engaging in a riot. Mr. Matthews could clearly see that riotous behavior and actions were escalating and ended up getting arrested with a bag of stolen liquor from a neighborhood store that was being looted.

(pauses for effect)

Mr. Matthews appealed the court's ruling but the charges were upheld, because the court determined there was no instance of constitutional deprivation and that the mere use of good judgement and socially acceptable behavior should have rendered a clear understanding that this was not acceptable behavior. In other words, it doesn't take a "rocket scientist" to figure out that a public riot is taking place and that the appropriate human response should be to stay at arm's length from the combustible situation.

(pauses for effect)

But, not only did the defendant, Dwayne LaFollett, not stay away from the combustible situation, his words and actions set it on **FIRE**!

LEONARD SNAYDER

Objection! Your Honor, counsel is leading the jury and using words out of context to color the opinion of the jury!

GRACE PORTER HAVERHILL

Sustained! Come on Mr. Pantovere, watch your wording!

MICHAEL PANTOVERE

I'm sorry your Honor, to rephrase, the defendant is of sound mind and body and it would seem that the ongoing occurrence of incidents of violence on the scene should have tempered his words and actions.

(pauses for effect)

A much more recent and troubling case involves the August 14, 2019 gathering of a group of activists and community members at the Pima County Adult Detention Complex in Arizona. They basically carried out a simple "noise demonstration" as a symbol of solidarity for the inmates to hear. They completed their demonstration and peaceably left the facility and then got arrested a mile away by the local sheriff's department.

(pauses for effect)

Reminiscent of your "J20" case, Judge, the now dubbed "Tucson 12" face felony rioting charges, a statute that hasn't been used for years in Arizona. Unfortunately, since the election of Donald Trump, anti-protest legislation has been appearing in statehouse agendas across the country. Coincidentally, two of the defendants in the "Tucson 12" case, were also apprehended in the "J20" case and both acquitted. It is again, simply a legal mechanism to discourage dissent. There is a difference between nonviolent civil disobedience and inflammatory speech and behavior resulting in imminent violence. The Supreme Court has placed great emphasis on the actual occurrence of violence after said words are spoken.

(pauses for effect)

My point here is that if local prosecutors and the Department of Justice are allowed to file these charges against defendants where there is no proof of any wrong doing, than we must be able to proceed and demand that the maximum sentence be handed down to the defendant, Dwayne LaFollett, for the part that he played on that fateful day here in Arlington, that resulted in such tragedy.

(pauses for effect)

On a final note, though it took over a year, in October 2018, four white supremacist participants of the Charlottesville, "Unite the Right" rally were finally each charged with one count of conspiracy to violate the federal riots act by the U.S. Attorney's Office in the Western District of Virginia. In July 2019, three of the four defendants were charged with prison sentences ranging from 27-37 months and could have faced fines of up to $250,000.

(pauses for effect)

Ladies and gentlemen of the jury, let me close by quoting Thomas Cullen, U.S. Attorney for the Western District of Virginia, who so eloquently stated, "The First Amendment protects an individual's right to speak, assemble, and espouse political views, but it does not license insensate acts of violence committed under the guise of First Amendment expression." **THIS ISN'T RIGHT VERSUS LEFT; IT IS RIGHT VERSUS WRONG!**

(pauses for effect)

We are asking that you, the jury, find the defendant, Dwayne LaFollett, guilty of disorderly conduct, as well as seventeen counts of violating the federal riots act and the intent to promote and encourage a riot, with the maximum 5-year prison sentence per count and the maximum $250,000 fine per count. The NRA has deep pockets and we are sure that they will help their esteemed leader foot the bill. It is your responsibility as a juror to weigh the facts here today and based on those facts, ask, how can anything but a guilty verdict be handed down? Thank you, I have nothing further.

Michael Pantovere takes his seat and Leonard Snayder stands.

GRACE PORTER HAVERHILL

Mr. Snayder, please proceed with your closing arguments.

LEONARD SNAYDER

Thank you, your Honor. Ladies and gentlemen of the jury, my client, Dwayne Lafollett, is saddened by the loss of life and for the injuries that occurred during the NRA rally, but in no way was he responsible.

(pauses for effect)

Ladies and gentlemen of the jury, let me call your attention to the rioting that occurred in the city of Baltimore, MD after the death of Freddie Gray and the very uneven **JUSTICE** for the rioters who were arrested in the aftermath. The city of Baltimore witnessed riots and protests for days and weeks, to the tune of $13.0 million in damages. At least 98 officers were injured with over 40 requiring hospitalization.

(pauses for effect)

The color of **JUSTICE** has consistently been a topic of unrest and protest in Baltimore. Approximately 550 people were arrested during this uprising in April/May 2015. Fewer than 100 were charged with any significant crime. One woman was held in jail on $50,000 bail for 7 months and then had all charges dropped against her. Bail amounts for those charged with

inciting a riot ranged from zero to $500,000 or
more.

(pauses for effect)

Of the 500+ arrested, only 79 were charged with
significant crimes. Half of the 79 defendant's
charges were dropped after being dragged through
the prosecutorial mud. 25 people received
convictions. One 22-year-old who was charged
with inciting a riot, disorderly conduct,
failure to obey and resisting arrest, was
committed to jail one day, given a $100,000 bail
the next day and then, the next day released on
his own recognizance. Case after case was
dropped. Then there was the man charged with a
4th degree burglary charge and $750,000 bail,
before charges being dropped. **JUSTICE** is all
over the map in Baltimore and we seem to be
following suit here in Arlington. Hundreds of
defendants were set free and yet, here is my
client, Dwayne Lafollett, fighting for his
rights, for his freedom, for **JUSTICE**!

(pauses for effect)

$13.0 million dollars in damages were sustained
as a result of the Baltimore riots after the
death of Freddie Gray and yet there were very
few consequences for those who participated.

MICHAEL PANTOVERE

Objection! Your Honor! I think we can all agree
that there has been an uneven scale of **JUSTICE**
in some of the arrests and sentencings in
Baltimore, not just in the Freddie Gray case,
but across the board, in other cases of civil
unrest and discrimination. Which can be blamed,

to some extent, on why the rioting surrounding the Freddie Gray case got so out of control. So, Mr. Snayder is correct in pointing out that the monetary damages incurred as a result of the rioting in Baltimore were excessive.

(pauses for effect)

But here today, we are talking about the loss of human life and mass injuries during the Arlington rally and in no way can you put a price tag on that! And yet, Dr. Mark Rosenberg, the former director of the U.S. Centers for Disease Control and Prevention's National Center for Injury Control and Prevention, did just that! His findings were that, "the federal government estimates that the value of a single human life is between $7 and $10 million. And that's just the monetary cost. For every person who is killed, you destroy a family and damage a community."

GRACE PORTER HAVERHILL

Sustained! Mr. Snayder?

LEONARD SNAYDER

Let me continue, by sharing another very recent charge of inciting a riot, against President Donald J. Trump. On March 1, 2016, then candidate Trump was presiding over a rally in Louisville, KY, where 3 protesters sustained injuries while being forcibly removed from the rally by Trump supporters. Candidate Trump verbally encouraged their removal, saying, "Get em outta here!" Resulting in some of the rally attendees forcibly removing the three from the premises.

(pauses for effect)

A federal trial court did allow the litigants to file charges against President Trump of, "inciting the crowd to violence against them." The President's lawyers tried to get the charges dropped, stating that his statements were directed towards security and also claimed that his speech was protected by the First Amendment, but the case was allowed to move forward.

(pauses for effect)

The challenge here was that it also had to be proven that the then, candidate Trump's **INTENT** was to incite violence and that's where the case fell apart and is also why this case has fallen apart. You cannot prove my client's **INTENT** was to incite a riot or any type of violent response. These are **EXACTLY** the instances where it is critical for First Amendment rights/free speech to be protected. Living in a **DEMOCRACY** allows for both sides to partake in rancorous debate. Everyone has a right to his or her own opinion and understanding of things. You don't have to agree. You just have to be willing to listen.

(pauses for effect)

The Federal Appeals Court ruled unanimously in favor of President Trump, stating that his words were protected by the First Amendment because, "he did not specifically advocate imminent lawless action." Also, in that he followed his initial statement of, "Get em outta here," with "Don't hurt em," it was ruled as a direct statement to spare violence or injury and the case was closed.

(pauses for effect)

Ladies and gentlemen of the jury, let me again stress that my client is deeply saddened by the senseless loss of life and injury, but if you cannot charge the President of our great country with inciting a riot, how can you allow these charges against my client?

MICHAEL PANTOVERE

Objection your Honor! For the record, ABC news recently conducted research which revealed that, at the time, there were at least 36 criminal cases where our "esteemed" President was "invoked in direct connection with violent acts, threats of violence or allegations of assault." As of December 2019, The Washington Post had calculated that President Trump had made 15,413 false or misleading claims since taking the oath of office. I will say it once more, **WORDS MATTER**!

CUT TO:

II.14 THE RED ROOM - SAME TIME

> *The room is darkened with s spotlight on Thomas Jefferson, who is intently watching the courtroom proceedings as they occur.*

THOMAS JEFFERSON

Nothing is so mistaken as the supposition, that a person is to extricate himself from a difficulty, by intrigue, by chicanery, by dissimulation, by trimming, by an untruth, by an

injustice. This increases the difficulties
tenfold; and those who pursue these methods, get
themselves so involved at length, that they can
turn no way, but their infamy becomes more
exposed.

                    (pauses for effect)

It is of great importance to set a resolution,
not to be shaken, never to tell an untruth.
There is no vice so mean, so pitiful, so
contemptible; and he who permits himself to
tell a lie once, finds it much easier to do it
a second and third time, till at length it
becomes habitual; he tells lies without
attending to it, and truths without the world's
believing him. This falsehood of the tongue leads
to that of the heart, and in time depraves all
its good dispositions.

                                          CUT TO:

II.15 INT. BACK TO COURTROOM - SAME TIME

                    GRACE PORTER HAVERHILL

Sustained! Thank you for sharing those facts,
Mr. Pantovere. Please continue, Mr. Snayder.

                    LEONARD SNAYDER

My client had no personal knowledge of, or any
type of interaction with the actual perpetrator,
Harrison Culpepper. He gave no type of personal
instruction to this crazed wife beater.
Unfortunately, no matter what words my client
spoke that day, the attack on our fine city
would have happened anyway. The great Henry
Ford, once said, "History is more or less bunk.

It's tradition. We don't want tradition. We want
to live in the present, and the only history
that is worth a tinker's dam is the history we
make today." You have the sacred responsibility
to find my client, Dwayne LaFollett, not guilty
of all charges. Thank you, your Honor. I have
nothing further. The defense rests.

GRACE PORTER HAVERHILL

Thank you, Mr. Snayder. Mr. Pantovere, any final
words?

MICHAEL PANTOVERE

Yes, your Honor. Again, I just have to
reiterate, there was no conspiracy charge filed
against the defendant. You cannot compare the
minor injuries sustained by three protestors at
a Trump rally to the death and mass injuries
sustained at the Arlington Rally. 17 people lost
their lives and another 203 were injured. There
is no reciprocity here. There just isn't.
Jurors, your responsibility is to review the
facts presented and FINALLY send the message
this country and our politicians need to hear.
Thank you, your Honor. Nothing further.

GRACE PORTER HAVERHILL

Ladies and gentlemen of the jury. You have now
been presented with the necessary evidence and
testimony, as presented by the prosecution and
the defense to commence deliberations on the
verdict for the defendant, Dwayne LaFollett ....

>   *As Grace continues to provide*
>   *instructions to the jury, you*
>   *hear a voice over the*

> *loudspeakers, providing some*
> *disturbing statistics*
> *resulting from some of the*
> *many mass shootings over the*
> *years in our country.*

                                    CUT TO:

II.16 THE RED ROOM - SAME TIME

> *Thomas Jefferson, George*
> *Washington, John Adams, and*
> *James Madison are standing or*
> *seated in various places*
> *around the room.*

                 THOMAS JEFFERSON

History, in general, only informs us what bad
government is.

                 JAMES MADISON

A bad cause seldom fails to betray itself.

                 JOHN ADAMS

It is a common observation in Europe that
nothing is so false as modern history. I should
add that nothing is so false as modern
history...except modern American history. It was
patched and piebald then, as it is now, ever
was, and ever will be, world without end.

                 GEORGE WASHINGTON

The Foundation of our Empire was not laid in the
gloomy age of Ignorance and Suspicion, but at an
Epoch when the rights of mankind were better

understood and more clearly defined, than at any former period. At this auspicious period, the United States came into existence as a Nation, and if their citizens should not be completely free and happy, the fault will be entirely their own.

THOMAS JEFFERSON

(said in a contemplative state as
he stares through the one-way
window into the courtroom)

Our desire is to pursue ourselves the path of **PEACE** as the only one leading surely to prosperity, and our wish is to preserve the morals of our citizens from being vitiated by courses of lawless plunder and murder.

(pauses for effect)

To you, then gentlemen, who are charged with the sovereign functions of legislation and to those associated with you, I look with encouragement for that guidance and support which may enable us to steer with **SAFETY** the vessel in which we are all embarked amidst the conflicting elements of a troubled world.

CUT TO:

ACT III

VINDICATION

III.1 INT. - COURTROOM - MORNING

> *There are throngs of*
> *protesters gathered outside*
> *the courtroom representing*
> *both sides of the argument,*
> *gun rights and gun control*
> *advocates. There is mass*
> *confusion and shouting, with*
> *each side holding banners*
> *espousing their views.*

BAILIFF

All rise. The Honorable Grace Porter Haverhill
is now presiding.

> *Grace enters the courtroom*
> *from her chambers, takes her*
> *seat, and POUNDS the gavel.*

GRACE PORTER HAVERHILL

Mr. Snayder and Mr. LaFollett, please stand and
face the jury.

> (pauses for effect)

Has the jury reached its verdict?

JURY FOREMAN

We have, your Honor.

GRACE PORTER HAVERHILL

What say you?

JURY FOREMAN

We, the jury, unanimously find the defendant,
Dwayne Lafollett, guilty of disorderly conduct,
as well as seventeen counts of violating the
federal riots act and the intent to promote and
encourage a riot as a result of the May 5, 2018
NRA rally here in Arlington, VA.

> Grace POUNDS the gavel and
> there is great excitement in
> the courtroom.

GRACE PORTER HAVERHILL

So be it recorded. In that there were seventeen
separate counts, one for each victim, was your
"guilty" verdict unanimous across all seventeen
counts or do we need to review each count
separately?

FOREPERSON

Unanimous for all counts, your Honor!

GRACE

Members of the jury hearken to your verdict as
the Court will record it. You, upon your oath,
do say that the defendant is guilty of
disorderly conduct and seventeen counts of
conspiracy to violate the federal riots act and
the intent to promote and encourage a riot? So
say you, Mr. Foreman? So say you, all members of
the jury?

FOREPERSON AND ALL JURORS

(Rise and speak in Unison)

We do, your Honor!

GRACE

Let the records show that the jury has returned, in total, seventeen guilty verdicts!

Grace POUNDS her gavel!

GRACE (CONT'D)

Sentencing will be handed down Monday, April 22nd, 2020, at 9:00 AM. Thank you, ladies and gentlemen of the jury. Your time and service are greatly appreciated. You may go home now!

BAILIFF

All rise.

> *Grace ceremoniously exits, amongst a great flurry of excitement. Snayder is trying to calm his client and Pantovere is looking content with the verdict as rendered.*

> CUT TO.

III.2 INT. - EARLY EVENING - THE HOME/DINING ROOM/LIBRARY OF JUDGE GRACE PORTER HAVERHILL AND HER HUSBAND DR. MITCHELL HAVERHILL

> *A very pregnant Grace Porter and husband Mitch are curled*

*up on the couch with a cup of
tea, discussing the events of
the day.*

                    GRACE PORTER HAVERHILL

So how was your first day of teaching at
Georgetown?

                    MITCHELL HAVERHILL

Great! I really enjoyed it and the students
seemed really into it! Just really engaging and
interesting conversation!

                    GRACE PORTER HAVERHILL

Ah, my brilliant shrink of a husband shaping
young minds.

I'm proud of you!

                    She kisses his forehead

                    MITCHELL HAVERHILL

And I'm proud of you! I like seeing your
beautiful face and big pregnant belly on the
news every day. Guilty on all counts! That was
quite the verdict!

                    GRACE PORTER HAVERHILL

Well, I'm sure they will appeal, regardless of
my sentencing. But I think it certainly sends a
message to gun rights groups and gun
manufacturers. It's a step in the right
direction.

(pauses for effect)

I've been thinking about names for the baby. If it's a girl, I really would like her middle name to be Gabrielle. How I wish she were still with us. She would have made such a fantastic aunt!

MITCHELL HAVERHILL

(said with some humor)

Yes, she would have. I think about her all of the time. Maybe not always such a great role model, but a great aunt for sure.

(pauses for effect)

Actually, even if we have a boy, his middle name could be Gabrielle or Gabe.

GRACE PORTER HAVERHILL

You're right! That's a great idea! First names for a girl, I was thinking maybe Anna, after my Mom, or Helen. I'd like for Helen to be the baby's God mother, if that's Ok with you?

MITCHELL HAVERHILL

Absolutely! If it's a boy, maybe we could name him Norman, after your Dad? I know that would mean a lot to you.

GRACE PORTER HAVERHILL

Really? You wouldn't mind?

MITCHELL HAVERHILL

Why would I mind? I think it would be great.
Let's call it a day! We both have big days ahead
of us tomorrow.

> *They both rise from the couch*
> *and exit.*

CUT TO:

III.3 INT. BACK TO COURTROOM - MORNING

> *There are throngs of*
> *protesters gathered outside*
> *the courtroom representing*
> *both sides of the argument,*
> *gun rights and gun control*
> *advocates. There is mass*
> *confusion and shouting, with*
> *each side holding banners*
> *espousing their views.*

BAILIFF

All rise. The Honorable Grace Porter Haverhill
is now presiding.

> *Grace enters the courtroom*
> *from her chambers, takes her*
> *seat, and POUNDS the gavel.*

GRACE

Please be seated. I want to thank you all for
your patience and use of sound judgment during
the proceedings of this trial. I am sure the
nature of this trial brought considerable angst
to many of you. The loss of seventeen lives,
especially under such brutal circumstances, is

never a pleasant consideration to be weighed
when deliberating the fate of another human
being. Yet you have done so and by a unanimous
verdict, found the defendant, Dwayne LaFollett,
guilty of disorderly conduct and all seventeen
counts of conspiracy to violate the federal
riots act and the intent to promote and
encourage a riot.

> (pauses for effect)

As is customary at the sentencing hearing,
Jackson Owens, the husband and father of four of
the deceased, will be given the opportunity to
make an impact statement. Are you ready, Mr.
Owens?

> JACKIE OWENS

Yes, your Honor.

> > *He stands and walks up to the*
> > *podium/microphone*
> > *ceremoniously.*

> JACKIE OWENS (CONT'D)

I stand here today in front of you, a man, but I
am a broken man!

> > *He starts shaking and trying*
> > *to hold back tears. He*
> > *continues to speak*
> > *passionately, waving a*
> > *photograph of his wife and*
> > *three children in the air.*

This **WAS** my family, **WAS MY FAMILY**! And now, I
have **NOTHING** left to live for except for the

hope to find some meaningful way to prevent this slaughtering from happening to another man and his **FAMILY**!

(pauses for effect)

So, I read the Bible a lot and I have been studying the words of Dr. King to somehow temper me from hate and hating, but it is not an easy task and I am not a perfect man. I copied down this quote from Dr. King, cause it is better than I can do and expresses my thoughts so well, he said, "To accept passively an unjust system is to cooperate with that system thereby the oppressed become as evil as the oppressor. Noncooperation with evil is as much a moral obligation as is cooperation with good."

(pauses for effect)

So, I stand here today before you a **HUMBLED MAN**, a **RIGHTEOUS MAN,** and a **BROKEN MAN** begging this court for a slice of redemption and to hand down a sentence that could help to discourage as many future mass shootings as possible. To hold the guilty accountable, and for we the people, to stand up and demand that our Congress and our states, open their eyes and start to value each and every life of our people and pass common sense legislation, including reinstating the military assault rifle ban **NOW**!

(pauses for effect and waves the picture of his family)

But don't do it for me, do it for them. Please do it for them!

He wipes the tears from his face and takes his seat

CUT TO:

III.4 THE RED ROOM - SAME TIME

> *Thomas Jefferson, George
> Washington, James Madison,
> John Adams, and Alexander
> Hamilton are seated or
> standing around the room,
> intently watching the
> courtroom proceedings through
> the one-way window.*

THOMAS JEFFERSON

When injustice becomes law, resistance becomes
duty!

JAMES MADISON

A pure Democracy can admit of no cure for the
mischiefs of faction. A common passion or
interest will, in almost every case, be felt by
a majority of the whole; a communication and
concert results from the form of government
itself; and there is nothing to check the
inducements to sacrifice the weaker party, or an
obnoxious individual.

(pauses for effect)

Hence it is, that such Democracies have ever
been spectacles of turbulence and contention;
have ever been found incompatible with personal
security, or the rights of property; and have in
general been as short in their lives, as they
have been violent in their deaths.

JOHN ADAMS

Remember democracy never lasts long. It soon wastes, exhausts, and murders itself. There never was a democracy yet that did not commit suicide.

(pauses for effect)

That the desires of the majority of the people are often for injustice and inhumanity against the minority, is demonstrated by every page of history in the whole world.

JAMES MADISON

On a candid examination of history, we shall find the turbulence, violence, and abuse of power, by the majority, trampling on the rights of the minority, have produced factions and commotions which, in republics, have, more frequently than any other cause, produced despotism.

GEORGE WASHINGTON

There is an opinion, that parties in free countries are useful checks upon the administration of the Government and serve to keep alive the spirit of **LIBERTY**. This within certain limits is probably true; and in Governments of a Monarchical cast, Patriotism may look with indulgence, if not with favor, upon the spirit of party.

(pauses for effect)

A fire not to be quenched, it demands a uniform vigilance to prevent its bursting into a flame, lest, instead of warming, it should consume.

JAMES MADISON

The **SAFETY** and happiness of society are the
objects at which all political institutions aim,
and to which all such institutions must be
sacrificed.

ALEXANDER HAMILTON

The vigor of government is essential to the
security of **LIBERTY**.

(pauses for effect)

Every man who loves, **PEACE**, every man who loves
his country, every man who loves **LIBERTY**, ought
to have it ever before his eyes, that he may
cherish in his heart a due attachment to the
Union of America, and be able to set a due value
on the means of preserving it.

GEORGE WASHINGTON

The preservation of the sacred fire of **LIBERTY**,
and the destiny of the Republican moral of
Government, are justly considered as deeply
perhaps as finally staked in the experiment
entrusted to the hands of the American people.

CUT TO:

III.5 INT. BACK TO COURTROOM - SAME TIME

GRACE PORTER HAVERHILL

Thank you, Mr. Owens. I know I can speak for
everyone in this courtroom today, when I say we
are truly sorry for your loss. And with that
being said, on behalf of your loved ones, who

were stricken down so senselessly, today, you are going to get more than thoughts and prayers.

(pauses for effect)

I've spent a great deal of time during the course of this trial studying recent statistics regarding guns, gun violence and mass shootings and though much I already knew or had heard of, there was some eye opening statistics and you've heard both counselors sharing statistics that favor their sides of the argument. However, there is one common thread woven among the statistics, regardless of what side of the argument you are on, and that is that **GUNS KILL**!

(pauses for effect)

And whether it is a single death or five or ten or seventeen or forty-nine, **IT IS TOO MANY**! Mr. Pantovere was right in his discussion regarding the safeguards required prior to individuals getting behind the wheel of an automobile, versus the somewhat limited safeguards required to buy an assault weapon, which as our case here today reminds us, took seventeen lives and injured over 200 in a matter of minutes. Come on people, come on Congress, we need to open our eyes and look at how badly this situation has spiraled out of control. If the New Zealand Prime Minister can pass a law in a week, certainly the United States can do so in a matter of **YEARS**!

(pauses for effect)

WE ARE KILLING EACH OTHER!!! You will never convince me that our founders could anticipate the advancements in weaponry and technology, that have resulted in such frequent occurrences

of mass casualties. In that he was British, one
might think that Winston Churchill would not
have held any fondness for the creation of our
Union, but actually, he loved America and even
referred to us as "his Americas!"

(pauses for effect)

In admiration he once said, "What body of men,
however farsighted, can lay down precepts in
advance for settling the problems of future
generations?" And there you have it. The
commonsense response to those who continue to
scream Second Amendment protection for their
arsenal of assault weapons and stockades of guns
that they stockpile in some exaggerated
expression of safeguarding themselves against
tyranny? Against their neighbor? Against their
spouse? Against their local law enforcement?

(pauses for effect)

It is safe to say that the gang violence issues
that have continued to proliferate in our
country over the last several decades, wouldn't
be as pronounced if there wasn't such easy
access to **GUNS**! We look at our neighbors, our
coworkers, people that we don't know and have
absolutely no reason to judge with distrust and
intolerance. Those were not the tenets that this
country was built upon. Article 1 of the 1948
United Nations, Universal Declaration of Human
Rights says, "All human beings are born free and
equal in dignity and rights. They are endowed
with reason and conscience and should act
towards one another in a spirit of **BROTHERHOOD**."
Words to live by, yet frequently forgotten.

(pauses for effect)

Please stand Attorney Snayder, Mr. LaFollett, I am ready to hand down your sentence.

                                        CUT TO:

III.6 THE RED ROOM - SAME TIME

> *Thomas Jefferson. George Washington, James Madison, John Adams, and Alexander Hamilton are seated or standing around the room, intently watching the courtroom proceedings through the one-way window.*

                JAMES MADISON

I go on this great republican principle, that the people will have **VIRTUE** and intelligence to select men of **VIRTUE** and wisdom. Is there no **VIRTUE** among us? If there be not, we are in a wretched situation. No theoretical checks, no form of government can render us secure. To suppose that any form of government will secure **LIBERTY** or **HAPPINESS** without any **VIRTUE** in the people is a chimerical idea.

            (pauses for effect)

If there be sufficient **VIRTUE** and intelligence in the community, it will be exercised in the selection of these men; so that we do not depend on their **VIRTUE**, or put confidence in our rules, but in the people who are to choose them. The institution of delegated power implies that there is a portion of **VIRTUE** and **HONOR** among mankind, which may be a reasonable foundation of confidence.

(pauses for effect)

This generation's elected legislators must heed to their senses and enact laws that safeguard the lives of their constituents and do so post haste! I will say it once more, the "character" of the Constitution must be tested by the experience of the future.

(pauses for effect)

Do not separate text from historical background. If you do, you will have perverted and subverted the Constitution, which can only end in a distorted form of illegitimate government.

James Madison exits the stage.

GEORGE WASHINGTON

A good moral character is the first essential in a man...It is therefore highly important that you should endeavor not only to be learned but **VIRTUOUS**. Our lady Grace is quite right in reminding us that this country was founded in the spirit of **BROTHERHOOD**!

George Washington exits the stage.

ALEXANDER HAMILTON

Natural **LIBERTY** is the gift of the beneficent Creator to the whole human race and that Civil **LIBERTY** is founded in that and cannot be wrested from any people, without the most manifest violation of **JUSTICE**.

Alexander Hamilton exits the stage.

THOMAS JEFFERSON

Having laboured faithfully in establishing the right of self-government, we see in the rising generation, into whose hands it is passing, that purity of principle and energy of character, which will protect and preserve it through their day and deliver it over to their sons as they receive it from their fathers.

> (pauses for effect and looking up to the heavens, as if for guidance)

Let these sons of today's turbulent world leave it a better place for their own sons, then how it was received by them from their fathers. **PEACE** and prosperity so visibly flowing from it have but strengthened our attachment to it and the blessings it brings, and we do not despair of being always a **PEACEABLE** nation.

> (pauses for effect)

How little do my countrymen know what precious blessings they are in possession of, and which no other people on earth enjoy.

> *John Adams walks over to Thomas Jefferson and places a hand on his shoulder, the stage darkens, shining a spotlight on Jefferson and Adams.*

THOMAS JEFFERSON (CONT'D)

Nothing...is unchangeable but the inherent and inalienable rights of man.

(pauses for effect)

God grant that men of principle shall be our principal men.

> Over loudspeakers in the
> background, echo loudly and
> repeat the words, "God grant
> that men of principle shall be
> our principal men," several
> times.

JOHN ADAMS

This country of our making is destined in Future history to form the brightest or blackest page, according to the use or the abuse of those political institutions by which they shall in time to come, be shaped by the human mind.

(pauses for effect)

You and I, my dear friend, have been sent into life at a time when the greatest lawgivers of antiquity would have wished to live. How few of the human race have ever enjoyed an opportunity of making an election of government, more than of air, soil, or climate, for themselves or their children!

When, before the present epocha, had three millions of people full power and a fair opportunity to form and establish the wisest and happiest government that human wisdom can contrive?

> (pauses for effect)

I hope you will avail yourself and your country
of that extensive learning and indefatigable
industry which you possess, to assist her in the
formation of the happiest governments and the
best character of a great people.

> *The stage goes dark. Over
> loudspeakers in the
> background, echo loudly and
> repeat the words, "the best
> character of a great people"
> several times.*

CUT TO

III.7 INT. BACK TO COURTROOM - SAME TIME

> *Grace POUNDS the gavel. There
> is much noise and excitement
> at the reading of her sentence!*

GRACE PORTER HAVERHILL

Order! Order in the court!

> (pauses for effect)

Mr. LaFollett, I have given great thought to the
severity of your sentence. I cannot use the
precedence recently set by the sentences handed
down to the three Charlottesville defendants
because they were intentionally, actively, and
willingly involved in physical acts of violence
and travelling in interstate commerce to do so.
However, they pled guilty to and were each only
charged with one count of conspiracy to riot
versus the seventeen charges that you have been
found guilty of, with no conspiracy charges, as

146

well as disorderly conduct, which is a much lesser charge.

(pauses for effect)

So, regarding the disorderly conduct charge, I am handing down the sentence of 30 days in jail and a $500 fine. However, for the seventeen counts of violating the federal riots act and the intent to promote and encourage a riot, my sentence is much greater.

(pauses for effect)

How can you place a value on the loss of a human life in terms of months in prison or monetary fines? It is a formidable consideration. The maximum per count prison time is five years.

I am certainly not going to give you an 85-year sentence, but I cannot let this reckless behavior continue. The disregard and casualness of encouraging and speaking words that can cause irreparable harm needs to stop. The First Amendment is not an absolute, nor is the Second Amendment.

(pauses for effect)

I am sentencing you to a half of a year in federal prison for each of the seventeen lives lost, which equals eight and a half years in prison.

However, the maximum monetary fine is $250,000 per count, which I am going to charge you with. $4,250,000 hardly seems to represent the value of seventeen lives lost. The severity of the crime certainly merits that amount. I sense you will easily be able to accommodate that amount.

(pauses for effect)

I hope that this sentence will begin to make others pause the next time they find themselves in a highly emotional public gathering and temper their words and their actions in an effort to promote **PEACE** and **DOMESTIC TRANQUILITY,** which is one of the most fundamental rights of the citizens of the United States of America.

(pauses for effect)

Mr. Owens, sir, again let me express my sincere condolences for your loss and for the losses of all of the other families and victims of this senseless tragedy. Hopefully, this will be seen as more than just thoughts and prayers and I hope it somehow brings you at least part of the redemption you need to move forward. George Will is one of my favorite contemporary journalists, I enjoy reading his columns and his books. He once said, "The business of America is not business. Neither is it war. The business of America **is JUSTICE** and securing the blessings of **LIBERTY**."

(pauses for effect)

Our founders did not lay down a framework to exonerate or minimize the severity of sentencings in response to the carnage of mass shootings. Of this, I am 100% sure. I sit here as a woman about to give birth and I am hoping that by the time my child or children reach school age, I will not need to be concerned about buying bullet proof backpacks and that our schools will no longer be customarily supplying their teachers and students with bleed out kits. Let us return to the civility that our founders

148

had in mind in the framing of our laws and in the founding of our great country. Let us leave here today in the spirit of **BROTHERHOOD**, assured that perhaps we are inching closer to regaining a sense of safety in our communities and **PEACE** in our hearts. Court is adjourned.

Grace POUNDS the gavel.

CUT TO:

III.8 INT. FLASHBACK - THE RED ROOM - SAME TIME

> *Show all of the founding fathers cheering with unanimous applause and patting each other on the backs in response to the courageous judge and her fiery sentence.*

CUT TO:

III.9 INT. BACK AT THE COURTROOM - SAME TIME

> *There is great applause in the courtroom and much excitement as the judge stands and makes her exit.*
>
> *Snayder is trying to calm his client and is assuring him that he will appeal on his behalf.*

CUT TO:

III.10 EXT. - EARLY EVENING - THE HOME/NURSERY
OF JUDGE GRACE PORTER HAVERHILL AND HER HUSBAND
DR. MITCHELL HAVERHILL - EVENING

> *Hear the sound of babies
> crying in the background. Show
> Mitch in front of a crib
> holding a baby dressed in blue
> and Grace in front of a crib
> holding a baby wearing pink.
> They walk towards each other
> and Mitch kisses Grace's
> forehead.*
>
> THE CURTAIN FALLS

CPSIA information can be obtained
at www.ICGtesting.com
Printed in the USA
LVHW091037091021
699992LV00001B/1